FROM A GREAT OAK..........

A LITTLE ACCOUNTANT GREW

By
Carol A. Beveridge

Published by
THE HEALING PLACE

Dedicated to Gordon, Judy and Mike
With much Love.

Copyright ©2000 Carol A Beveridge

First published in 2000 by The Healing Place
Ettrick Bank, Ettrickbridge, Selkirk TD7 5JL
All Rights Reserved

No part of this publication may be reproduced or transmitted in any form or by any means without the prior permission in writing from the author.

A catalogue record for this book is available from The British Library.

ISBN 0 9538691-0-5

Printed for The Healing Place by
Meigle Printers Ltd
Tweedbank Industrial Estate
Galashiels

PROLOGUE

The ice had gone but there was that bright freshness to the morning. Everything was still and very very quiet. In the silence, a branch of a tree quivered—all else was motionless—nothing was there—every other branch was undisturbed. There were no birds about. There was an energy—a mistiness—a hint of colour in that small section of the tree—an area of warmth—indeed the silvery trace which still clung to all the other branches was no longer present on this high branch of the oak tree. It was as if something or someone had been sitting here looking down on the quiet scene below.

What might they have been watching....? A grey roadway—a few parked cars—a terrace of houses—a few run-down shops and a middle aged business man....

The oak tree was fairly large and quite impressive as it stood alone on a tiny grassy area in front of a row of neat single storey dwellings—a line up of small homes adjoining each other—all exactly the same at first glance—one door one window—one door one window all along the line, all painted the same—all in the same state of repair. These must be council owned—maintained by the same set of hands—the same tins of green paint. But wait! There were some differences—some individuality when you really looked. Two houses in particular had a marked contrast. One house had no net curtains and had a bright pair of orange—yes, orange curtains. Could it be that these small orange curtains seemed to make this particular house stand out from all the rest?

The house on the left was just like all the others—no difference there—no contrast. But the house on the right—the last in the row—what was different here....? This house seemed lower, as if the last soldier in the rank had sunk into the mud—his shoulders hunched, his being broken by an invisible weight on his young shoulders.

This house or its occupant carried such a burden. The end house was in fact, exactly the same as all the others in its proportions and physical attributes. There was no subsidence—no hidden underground collapse. It was just a house of great sadness bearing the darkness of desperate despair.

This was number eight Oak Walk—the home—no, not a home—the place where Harry Boswell—widower—aged eighty-seven lived or rather existed.

Next door—at number seven, behind the bright orange curtains, lived his neighbour, Henry MacFarlane—also a widower, aged eighty-seven.

The smartly dressed businessman had lingered for a few moments under the oak tree that morning. His attention had been drawn to whatever had taken place high in these branches. His eyes had observed the movement, the mistiness—the colour and the warmth. He had been affected by this altered energy. He did not know it, but his life would never be the same again.

His name was James Jeremiah Fanshaw.

ONE

I looked up again. In the high branches of the oak tree I was able to make out the area on the tree that was different—some warmer presence had rested there.

The sun had not yet reached this area. I knew that something special lingered there. I also knew that its attention had been directed at this row of houses and, in particular, at the end house—number eight.

This house, or its occupant, had been under the scrutiny of this—I did not know what.

As I stood under the oak tree, I felt that I too had been affected by this strange phenomenon. There was a sense of synchronicity. I was part of a much bigger picture. Like those branches untouched by frost, I too was warmed and influenced by unseen fingers and a new vibration.

When I look back on this moment I was aware that some change had taken place in me—what the change was I could not say. I seemed able to trust, with an inner certainty, that this was so and my mental powers and logical mind were of no relevance.

I felt remarkably calm and untroubled, free of questions or doubts. It was as if an invisible doorway had opened and revealed a lighted pathway stretching out before me.

There was no blinding flash—no earth shattering revelation—just a melting of frost—a quivering vibrational change—a lightness—a feeling of purpose. I was an instrument in some future plan.

It was as if an angel had touched my shoulder!

I had walked past this corner of the town hundreds of times over the years but somehow had never really noticed it. I remembered this row of sheltered housing being built and had a vague memory of a petition to save a tree when the builders were clearing the site. I had been young then and it had been of little interest to me. I felt glad that people had cared enough to save it. I reached out and touched the huge trunk—my fingers tingled inside my gloves—instinctively I moved closer and rested my back against the tree.

I was not a tree hugging, green sort of person—at least not until now—I was a middle aged accountant who dealt in figures and practicalities—stock markets and tax returns—really important things that made sense and could be proved.

I had entered a new exciting dimension—my perspective had changed that morning. I had discovered a depth of sensation I had never known before.

I felt part of this tree. I closed my eyes and listened and felt and smelt and tasted this moment.

This triangle of grass, at the edge of the road, was empty apart from the tree and three randomly placed benches all of differing design. Each bench had a brass plaque screwed to its back panel. They were probably memorials—reminders of former residents of these houses. The houses had no gardens, so this green space would be a welcome place for the residents to sit during the summer months and this huge oak tree, when in leaf, would give a welcome shelter from the hot sun. I felt a wave of immense gratitude to these conservationists who had taken the time to save this tree.

My eyes went back to the row of houses. The two at the end were the ones which held my attention. As I watched, the orange curtains moved. They were pushed open slowly—first the right hand one then the left. A face peered through the window—a round pleasant face with large glasses. He leant forward towards the glass pane and really looked out. I felt he was taking in everything—this scene which he looked at every day—he would know if anything had changed. This was a man who used his senses, who had great awareness and who appreciated things. This elderly man was welcoming the new day—grateful possibly that he had another day to experience. I could not make out his features but I felt that he was smiling and bidding the outside world a cheerful good morning.

Next door, at number eight, nothing moved, yet I knew that behind these colourless curtains, someone was awake and facing a new day. As I focused on this dwelling—exactly the same structurally as the house next door—my new awareness gave me a feeling of being pulled down—an anguish—a despair. I was engulfed in a darkness—a black heaviness—a choking suffocation.

These two houses were as contrasting to me as a neat set of accounts and a pile of shoe boxes crammed with a mass of crumpled and torn receipts and invoices.

With my skills I could put the latter in good order. It would take many hours of painstaking endeavour but I could do it. However the problems that lay inside Number Eight Oak Walk were far beyond the abilities of this middle aged accountant....

Reluctantly I began to move away from the oak tree and proceeded towards my office.

I had been, until now, a man of order, routine and regime. A man people could set their watches by—a man who was predictable and probably rather boring.

I had begun this thirty minute walk, at the start and finish of each working day, about a month ago after a routine health check revealed an increase in my cholesterol level. From that time I had made adjustments to my daily routine to accommodate this exercise plan along with a new dietary regime of low fat and more fruit.

As I walked back, I was aware that my senses were still sharper. I seemed more aware of everything—my feet inside my shoes as they touched the pavement, the movements of my arms and legs—the cool air on my face—the varied sounds of the passing traffic and the hurrying people all around me.

To my knowledge until that morning I had never walked along Oak Walk. What, I wondered, had changed that morning to alter my pattern and take me this way? My routine was the same each morning—down Lavender Close, round the park, across the canal bridge and back by the post box on Holy Corner. However, that morning workmen had begun digging up the road and footpath in order to lay cable TV along Cavener Street and cutting across by the old folks' houses had been the obvious by-pass to this obstruction. I mused on this coincidence as I made my way towards the office.

I still did not feel quite myself as I stepped through my door into the front office. The secretaries, Fiona and Julia, looked at me strangely. Could they, I wondered, see a change in me? On my desk a cup of black tea was cooling and to my horror the clock on the wall read nine thirty! Never in twenty five years had I been late for work!

A few minutes later there was a soft tap on my office door and a hesitant voice said, "Mr. Fanshaw, I've brought you a fresh cup of Earl Grey. That one will be cold by now."

"Thank you, Julia." I beamed at her. She looked surprised and rather uncomfortable. "I've been thinking," I heard myself say, "We need to brighten up these offices. Orange curtains? What do you think? And perhaps a few house plants! See what you and Fiona can do."

As she left I heard her burst into the outer office and say to Fiona, "You won't believe it—the old man's finally flipped—He wants orange curtains and plants to brighten up the office! Whatever's got into him? And he's smiling! Do you think I need to put his name down for Oak Walk?"

"Beside my Bert's grandad you mean? He's at number eight—a right miserable old sod he is. He's never been the same since Bert's gran died. He's just given up. You wouldn't get a smile out of him, I can tell you." This was Fiona's voice.

So, Fiona in my office, was married to the grandson of the occupant of that house! Well I never!....

TWO

I didn't feel I was teetering on the edge of senility as Julia seemed to think—the reverse was nearer the truth. I felt younger and more alive. I was fifty seven years old and I had in this time been in and out of perhaps three, what might be called significant relationships. I had enjoyed periods of happiness and also endured times of sadness and heartbreak. At that time I was experiencing a time of quiet orderliness, living quite contentedly on the periphery of life. My personality sought order and stability and I had decided that the person I was, existed most peacefully and harmoniously in a single household. I felt safe when things were programmed and unadventurous. I shied away from impulsiveness and preferred my life to be like my ledgers, neat and orderly.

All my life I had tended to stay safely within my comfort zones and was fearful and hesitant of change. I didn't like to think about or talk about feelings. I did no one any harm. I gave to charity in a tax deductible sort of way but I would never have dreamt of doing anything for charity—good works, that sort of thing.

I loved my work and was passionate about it. Figures and finance excited and enthralled me and I ran a small but successful business. Until that moment under the oak tree I had felt fulfilled and content with my life.

Now all of a sudden, I was beginning to "feel" things. It was as if I had been living inside a shell and all at once the shell had expanded—moved outwards all around me, and left me with this extra layer of sensation, of energy, of knowing.

I suppose it might have been compared to a man who had been paralysed all his life being able to walk or a blind man now having sight, only this was more subtle. I didn't know what this change would allow me to do nor where it might lead me.

I felt excited and exhilarated as I mused over my cup of Earl Grey and considered the strange events of the morning.

The loud ringing of the telephone brought me back to accountant mode with a jerk. I was back within my comfort zone focused and ordered for the time being but there was a warm glow deep inside reminding me that there was more, much much more to discover.

I had changed from that moment under the oak tree but it was no immediate, Road To Damascus, type of experience. I was not a completely different man from that moment. The changes seemed to come and go in little glimmers of awareness and a slow deepening impression of seeing a broader more expansive picture.

My hearing was not suddenly more acute but I slowly realised that I was hearing on a different level—trivialities would catch my attention—I would pick up passing remarks and innuendos. Words and sounds which until then had passed me by now started to hold my attention. I became eventually a silent observer—gathering and collecting and storing words and expressions relating to feelings.

That spring I heard the dawn chorus—the first cuckoo, children's laughter, a client's breathing altering or a tremor in a stranger's throat. I began to hear how a person was feeling.

My eyesight did not suddenly become twenty-twenty vision, but I did, very very slowly over that summer, see so much more, a wider richer deeper picture. Colours were never so bright, contrasts of light and shade so exciting. I saw with delight, tiny snowdrops, raindrops on the dark green rhododendron leaves, hidden tears, faces alight with laughter.

I began to touch things—the smoothness of polished wood, the texture of cloth, the softness of the moss on the riverbank, the coolness of the river water as it moved over my fingers, the warmth of the sun as it came up on a summer morning at dawn.

I smelt the pizza delivery boy's box as he went past. I smelt the unwashed rawness and the alcohol on the old man who sold papers outside the station. I smelt home-made jam as I walked past Mrs. O'Conner's door that July.

All my senses had suddenly been switched on and gradually, very very gradually I became aware of what had happened to me and I began to delight in this new and exciting transformation. It was as if I had been connected up to a multitude of new channels of information. This was to me more wonderful than linking in to the internet or the wonders of cable television.

I became fascinated with people and how they interacted. I had never before analysed how I was feeling far less wondered how other people were feeling.

I watched and listened. I was like a sponge soaking up every emotional interchange. I felt a bit like an alien newly arrived from another planet, gathering information about these beings living on planet Earth. This is exactly how it was—I did want to know how other people, feeling people, saw the world and reacted in it.

With my heightened awareness I began my research. I eavesdropped shamelessly. I would leave my office door ajar so that I could hear the girls' conversations. A whole new world began to unfold. What lives they lived—it was a revelation! It was several weeks before I realised that most of the dramas I heard being discussed were not their personal intrigues or those of their friends or neighbours but belonged to the fantastical world of the television and its many soap operas. As a result of this, I began to tune in regularly to these kitchen sink dramas and watch the extremes of emotions enacted over and over again.

If I had lived within a family the changes in me that year would have been noticed but as it was, it was only Fiona and Julia in the office who saw me every day and they probably always thought me rather odd.

The orange curtains and the plants did brighten up the office and other little touches were added by the girls over the months that followed. When I look back I realise that my relationship with the staff mellowed and by the following Christmas they were relaxed enough with me to give me a "Mr. Happy" china mug and I used this instead of the bone china cups and saucers—these were then only used when clients shared tea or coffee with me. That gift gave me so much pleasure—my new feelings were up and running by then and I was able to express my delight when I opened their gift. I hadn't reached hugging yet but I certainly beamed with pleasure and laughed in delight as I thanked them.

THREE

During the weeks that followed that morning under the oak tree, I was drawn back there over and over again. I wanted to relive the experience—see it again—prove to myself it hadn't been a figment of my imagination. On my walks I always dallied under the oak tree and when the weather became warmer I would often sit on one of the benches on this grassy corner in front of the old folks' houses. Had it been a school or a children's playground I would probably have been reported to the police as an unsavoury man—a deviant of some kind. Fortunately no one thought me a threat to the residents of Oak Walk.

I maintained a keen interest in the two houses at the end of the row. The contrast between the two was as great as ever.

The bright orange curtains, which had prompted my changes at the office, were always opened wide. The dull grey ones next door were only ever parted by an inch or two, that is if they opened at all.

For many months I never saw sight nor sound of Mr. Boswell at number eight. Whenever anyone called at his door it opened only a fraction. If anyone entered they pushed the door ajar themselves as they went in.

The gentleman at number seven, next door, opened his door wide and ushered visitors in. He was delighted to welcome everyone and would, I felt sure, be a perfect host. His callers all looked brighter as they left, nourished in some way. Children would wave and call out to the friendly man in number seven. Birds watched his door and flew down to be fed. Postmen, milkmen and delivery men stopped and chatted at this door but moved quickly away from the door of number eight.

It amused me to observe the behaviour of the different meals on wheels ladies, as they delivered warm foil trays to these two houses. They obviously took it in turns and alternated between the two doors. Their demeanour told me which house they had been allocated as soon as they left the van. It was as if the one heading for Mr. Boswell's door had shrunk several inches. I could feel the heavy invisible armour she had put around herself and recognise the determined stride as she approached the door.

Here was an old campaigner. She had long given up the cheery—'How are we today?' approach—This was a—'Here you are, take it or leave it—get me out of here'—delivery! She glanced enviously at her companion as she, with a lightness of step and a genuine smile almost danced towards the neighbouring doorway and the pleasant man who waited there full of grateful thanks and polite appreciation. This was what the job was meant to be like. As they returned to the van it appeared as if one volunteer had been kissed and the other slapped. Next day the roles would be reversed.

When it was the turn of a new volunteer and she was unprepared for her first visit to number eight, the affect was even more dramatic. She would jauntily approach the door full of goodwill and cheery greeting and exit deflated and squashed like an old crumpled balloon. She would be either downcast and grey like a child who has been rejected and knocked back in a moment of eager enthusiasm, or else fiery and angry with a mouthful of colourful expletives directed at Mr. Boswell's parentage.

It was apparent that the resident of number eight Oak Walk was a thoroughly disagreeable old man.

The man in number seven, I was sure had noticed me on that first morning, as he pulled open his orange curtains to welcome the day. His piercing eyes would not have failed to observe a stranger standing so close to the trunk of the oak tree so early on a cold morning. I wondered if he also noticed a certain lightness in one area of the branches above my head. I felt, indeed I almost knew, that he had.

I had become a familiar figure in Oak Walk by the time the resident of number seven and I spoke for the first time. We had exchanged a smile and a nod many times as I walked past his window on the chill dark mornings into early spring.

Had he, I wondered, noticed the changes in me? These changes were not all internal, they had spilled over into my outward appearance—I became less formal and more relaxed in the way I dressed, though in the office I still wore a shirt and tie and polished shoes and a suit—but I was becoming less predictable and safe.

One day, a warm spring day, I was seated on one of the benches daydreaming, having eaten a lunch of salami sandwich on brown bread and enjoyed a black cherry yoghurt and a banana. I had closed my eyes and was listening to the sounds of the birds, the gentle hum of the lunch time traffic and the slight movement of the wind in the new green leaves of the oak tree. I felt very content and at peace with the world.

Suddenly I felt that I was no longer alone and opened my eyes. The old man from number seven was beaming down on me—a face as warm and bright as the sunshine. The eyes were blue—I knew they would be—alert and laughing—eyes that saw everything. His glasses were large and seemed to keep slipping forward on his nose. He leant quite heavily on a walking stick—a plane wooden stick with a rubber knob on the end—the kind they give out at the Aids department at the hospital—that's what they used to call it. I expect they have had to give it a new name now!

The old man lowered himself carefully down beside me. "Henry MacFarlane," he said. "Enjoying the sunshine are you? Not disturbing you I hope?"

"Not at all," I said, moving up the bench to make more room for the old man. "I am James Fanshaw. Hope you don't mind me using your bench. It's such a welcome corner. I've become quite attached to it and this beautiful tree."

"I've noticed. You come here a lot. You interest me, James Fanshaw," he said looking me straight in the eye.

"And you me," I replied returning his smile.

There was a respect and fascination between the two of us.

Over the months, bit by bit, I learned more and more about Henry MacFarlane and how he had become this joy of a human being. A man who seemed to glow with an inner knowing—a certainty—a man who lived very much in the present moment—a man who was completely at peace with his surroundings, his world, his fellow man and most importantly of all, himself.

Being in his presence was a fulfilling experience—becoming his friend, which I eventually felt I was—was one of the greatest gifts I ever received.

In the beginning we merely exchanged pleasantries but as the summer days lengthened and our times on the bench became more frequent, I slowly learned more and more about the turning on of the light within Henry MacFarlane.

FOUR

Henry's life had been fairly ordinary in the beginning. A normal kind of childhood—if there is such a thing—unremarkable, might be a better word.

He fell in love with Alice when they were both still at school. They courted, married and settled contentedly into a comfortable home life. Henry worked in a local factory. It made cardboard boxes.

He and Alice had two sons four years apart. First there was James—he would have been two years older than me if he had lived—Henry's eyes moistened, and he went quiet for a while, when he reached this part of his story. We sat silently and I felt his pain.

Henry continued his story. "Then there was Matthew. Two lovely lads so different in looks and temperament. Our home was like everyone else's—a mixture of joy, laughter, anger and squabbling, raised voices and stubborn moods.

James was the athletic one—good at all sports—a really wonderful eye for the ball. He was always in a rush—keenly competitive, hating to lose. He was volatile but didn't harbour a grudge. Everyone loved James—he had lots of friends and Matthew worshipped him when they were little and envied him his outgoing personality as they grew older.

Matthew was more introverted and sensitive. He was the most good hearted child as I recall. I think James took advantage of this at times.

Alice was a capable wife and an excellent mother and she was content and fulfilled in this role. Her boys meant the world to her.

Our lives seemed nicely worked out. We were content with what we had."

Henry stopped for a few minutes and then went on to tell me how, in an instant, their cosy world was shattered for ever. All had been in perfect order in the morning.... How he had relived that normality over and over again in his mind—the rush of breakfast in a busy household. The boys irritating each other—normal bickering as they gathered their school books and games kit together—pouring cereal, demanding things from their willing adoring mother.

That morning had been magnified somehow—every trivial detail—a sort of focus for later. The cornflakes had run out—Matthew had finished them—his bowl overly filled—much to his brother's annoyance. James was making a fuss—no other cereal would do—he'd particularly wanted cornflakes that morning. Alice was fussing around offering toast or eggs. Henry just wanted to escape to get away to the quiet orderliness of his office. He left them all to it, little knowing these were to be their last minutes together as a family.

By four o'clock that afternoon their lives were in pieces—things would never be the same again. They never could be.

Even after all these years Henry was still reliving that terrible day as he recounted the events to me. My eyes filled with tears as his normally strong voice broke and shook for a moment. Then the facts, plain and unadorned, like a news reader's report, gave me the stark story.

There are no words to describe such a time in any father's life.

James had been at football practice at school. He suddenly fell over and died—his heart just stopped. A heart defect which had gone undetected since birth.

"Natural Causes," Henry went on, "the coroner said ... I remember hearing these words at the inquest and wanting to scream out in rage that there was nothing normal or natural about it—my beautiful, full of life son was dead!"

As Henry said these words there was no rage in his voice just a deep deep sadness. He continued his story after a pause.

"From the moment of James' death the light inside me seemed to die. I withdrew into a dark tunnel and wrapped myself in its darkness. I went through the motions of living. People said how well

I was coping. I carried on—back to work, supporting Alice and Matthew. My feelings had been put on hold. They were turned off. I was on automatic pilot, working purely on the superficial. I remained like this for four or five years. I closed down emotionally leaving Matthew and Alice to handle their own pain.

The days and weeks came and went. The house was quiet—no rows, no arguments, no teasing, no jokes. We watched television, went to things at Matthew's school, went on holiday, went shopping, painted the house, did the garden, celebrated birthdays, Christmases and anniversaries. Those years were colourless.

I realised later how hard this time was for Alice and Matthew. We eventually talked about and were able to share our memories of this time, our experiences and our deep hurts.

In all grieving situations, each person's pain and ways of handling it is different.

Matthew says he felt heavily burdened with the responsibility of making up for the loss of James to us. He felt he had to be a super-perfect son, yet felt incapable of filling the enormous void James had left. He wasn't James and would never be the person James had been.

Matthew might well have gone off the rails at this time but instead, he hid away in his books and studied hard. I suppose in a way he switched off too.

Alice had her way of coping too. She threw herself into good works—helping everyone. She wore herself out running after other people and I suppose hid her feelings of loss in other people's problems and pain.

It was many years later before I was ready and able to share emotions with Matthew and Alice. It was a wonderfully cleansing and healing time when I could eventually hold, each in turn, and tell them how sorry I was and how much I loved them both.

Matthew and I are close now, but somehow, the damage which was done to both of us and especially to Matthew, who was, in a sense, an emotional orphan from the age of thirteen to eighteen, has left a deep wound, which though healed on the surface, still has scar tissue underneath.

Not surprisingly, he is very self assured and in command of himself. He got a good degree and has done very well in the world of banking. He is now in Australia—managing a large bank in Melbourne. He has, as far as I know, had a successful marriage and has raised three attractive, well balanced children.

He keeps in touch—writes occasionally and rings up fairly regularly. He has been very attentive since his mother died five years ago. He tries to manage over to see me once a year.

I am very fortunate. I have a wonderful son in Matthew."

Henry and I sat quietly for a while—each pondering on what had been said. I felt privileged to have been allowed to share in these innermost, deeply personal and emotional moments. Henry, I think, was wondering why he had felt the need to go over it all again with such a recent acquaintance. It was an emotional yet comfortable silence and we both felt a sort of bond and strange commitment to this growing friendship.

We again lost ourselves in silence. Henry, I imagined, was looking deep within, remembering. I became aware that I had opened up a so far untapped part of myself. This was the first time anyone had shared with me their deep emotional issues. Was this really the case, I wondered, or was it that this was the first time I had heard and empathised with someone else's feelings and shared in their pain? Had there perhaps been other occasions where I had been in similar positions and just perceived it all differently in a superficial, uninvolved sort of way—my mind analysing and my heart untouched? I probably always looked at such a story as I would a mess of financial chaos—separating off the top layer—the data the tax man needed to know.

That day was my first real feeling of empathy—a sharing of feelings and emotions. Henry had been able to see this in me and allowed me this experience. I felt a huge debt of gratitude to this elderly man.

I felt Henry's eyes upon me. It was as if he knew exactly what I was thinking. I sensed an imperceptible nod and a hint of a smile on his lips. Our eyes met—there were no words to express what happened in this moment but a communication took place.

I had questions clamouring inside my head but these were for another time.

Henry got up and slowly and arthritically, he made his way to his front door. My eyes followed him until he disappeared indoors without a backwards glance.

I remained on the bench—analysing this new level of awareness which I had discovered in myself. My eyes went up to the branches of the oak tree high above my head—that area which had caught my attention all those weeks ago. I knew with a profound inner confidence that this held the key—this was where all these changes in me had begun. I didn't understand it. I could not explain it, but I knew it to be so. It felt as if I was caught up in something—this was not all about me … was perhaps, the tree or Henry, a sort of catalyst? I was not able to find an answer then and it did not seem to matter.

FIVE

It was quite a time until I spoke to Henry again. I could not get him out of my mind and found myself listening over and over in my head to his story. I needed time to do this.

The weather had changed—it was wet and cold. I was anxious to meet up with Henry but circumstances, or some guiding hand, kept us apart.

I still walked past the oak tree at least once a day but was unable to linger there because of rain or business commitments. I was like a child being thwarted from having a treat—waiting for Christmas morning or for a birthday surprise.

It must have been about three weeks later when the gods smiled on me—the sun was shining and I had no appointments over lunch time. There was a lightness in my step as I made my way to the bench on Oak Walk, clutching my plastic tupperware box containing my lunch. I was convinced that Henry would join me on the bench. I smiled to myself—It must look as if I am on my way to meet a secret lover. It did feel a bit like that. How often that word 'feel' seemed to crop up these days!

I sat and took in the now familiar scene. The oak tree was in full leaf—a wonderful green canopy above my head. The houses were much the same. Henry's door stood open wide and Mr. Boswell's tightly shut—a two inch space showing between his drab curtains. A great sadness fell over me as I watched this grey corner house and I closed my eyes.

Suddenly I became aware of Henry standing beside me—the sad unhappy feeling lifted. I moved up and Henry lowered himself carefully into the space next to me, propping his stick against the edge of the bench.

"I've missed you." He said.

I smiled, a warm glow inside me. I didn't need to say anything. He knew.

"I've been wondering," I said after a few minutes, "about what you told me. What happened to bring you back—out of the dark place—years after your son died?"

My question sounded rather direct and intrusive but Henry did not seem to notice and answered straight away.

"This is a question I've often asked myself over the years. There was no one thing—no startling flash of light—no miracle healing." He smiled gently and said, almost to himself "I sometimes think perhaps an angel touched my shoulder." He went quiet for a moment—musing on this thought, then continued in his normal voice.

"These years after James died were so strange. I felt a light inside me had been turned off—now I realise that it had not been switched off—just turned down very very low, leaving a tiny pilot light inside a dirty grey shade, waiting for the time when an invisible hand—a breath of wind—a flake of snow, would begin to turn up that dimmer switch. That's how it was—as if a dimmer switch began to make very slow, hesitant turns. It was so gradual I was unaware for a long time, that changes were occurring. That switch is still turning and will continue to do so until it reaches the brightest light of all…." He paused again—a dreamy joyful look on his face for a moment. His eyes clouded as he continued.

"That grey time in my life is so hard to look back on. I wasn't in a black pit of depression. There was no black just interminable greyness. Dark grey—no contrasts, no light or shade—no colour. It was as if someone had left dark grey paint on all the colours in my paint box—so when I dipped my brush in the pot marked blue, it came out grey—all the colours in the paint box were the same.

It was the same with all my senses—all sounds were the same dull tempo—no rise or fall. Voices were monotonous and dull. Tastes were all the same—bland, insipid—neither pleasant nor unpleasant. I didn't feel hot or cold. The days were neither good nor bad. Nothing upset me nothing excited me.

What you have to realise, James," he went on, "I wasn't, at that time aware of any of this—I didn't realise that I was only half alive. I didn't know that I was in this dark place—I was just getting on with things as best I could.

If you don't feel—don't register emotions, you don't realise that you are sad, you don't know that your life is impoverished.

It wasn't until the light had turned up sufficiently for me to see my new experiences that I became aware of how much had been lacking in my life.

My 'lighting up' was slow and very very gradual", explained Henry. "This is not always the case. For some it may happen suddenly—out of the blue—more of a blinding flash—perhaps brought about by an illness—an accident—redundancy—a relationship breakdown—whatever—some sort of life crisis. Others get a less dramatic wake-up call—a slow dawning—an inner knowing—a mystical experience—a spiritual awakening.

Sometimes this wake-up call is for you alone—another time it may also be a wake-up call for someone else. You may be the catalyst in the awakening of another person. You are awakened at a particular time for a purpose as if you are somehow on a mission....!"

Henry always seemed to know when to stop in his conversations with me. He would drop so much into my lap then leave me to work with it—mull it all over and, when the time was right we would meet up again and he would offer me my next seed of enlightenment.

This was disconcerting at first. Henry would suddenly in the midst of a conversation start to move—edging forward and with two or three swaying movements of his upper body and a push with one hand, he was on his feet and on his way home.

We seldom had any words of greeting or farewell. This normally would have seemed odd—almost rude—but somehow it didn't—this was just how it was between Henry and me!

He had given me much to think about and I sat on awhile musing over what he had said to me. I felt his words held some important message and I knew he had left me to sort it all out in my mind.

Henry knew, and now I knew that I had had a wake-up call and with a deep inner knowing I knew this call was not just for me. I was on some kind of mission. I was equally certain that Henry knew what this mission was and that he would not tell me what it entailed—enough that he had let me know it was there.

I would not talk with Henry again until I had discovered for myself what all this was about and had some insight into what was planned for me.

For many days and at times when wakeful in the night, I searched my mind for answers. I put my intense analytical accountant's mind to the task. I fretted and I agonised and I progressed nowhere. I felt restless and frustrated and had become an insomniac.

One night, as I lay awake, I was struck by the sudden realisation that I was trying too hard. Had I learned nothing at all over these last months? I eventually challenged myself with this question. This was not a task for the mind—the intellect—the logic. I had to go back to the beginning—do nothing—wait and trust. This realisation was a breakthrough in itself and I slept peacefully at last.

I rose very early next morning refreshed and eager to be outdoors—exercising not only my body but also my senses.

It was a cool misty morning, the kind that holds the promise of a beautiful summer's day. I could smell that promise in the chilly mist as it touched my face with damp fingers. I walked quickly and purposefully.

The town was still asleep, only the early morning workers were about—postmen, newsagents, milkmen and bakers. I found myself in my usual place on the bench under the oak tree. All the houses were silent—curtains still tightly drawn. The orange curtains were closed but I suspected that Henry would know that I was here. I sat back and waited—looking for some sign. Nothing moved. The grass was heavy with dew. Droplets glinted and sparkled on each tiny blade. Cobwebs were transformed into pieces of intricate lace. There was an air of expectancy in the air—or perhaps within me.

A sleek tortoiseshell cat moved purposefully across the area of green, leaving tiny footprints in its wake. Her direction did not waver. She knew exactly where she was heading—"she's on a mission." I thought. She disappeared between two houses at the far end of the street.

I looked around again. A post-van had stopped beside the red pillar box on the far pavement. The postman's keys jangled noisily as he opened the box and raked out the letters from inside. These letters knew where they were going—their directions were clearly written on their envelopes—no wondering doubt for them.

I felt my attention being drawn to the oak tree. I stared up into the wide branches covered in wet leaves. The highest branches were shrouded in mist. I gasped as I became aware that one area was free from the blanket of mist. It was as if there was a warm area again—just like that first time, when the frost melted from one particular branch.

I got up and walked back from the tree—it must have been a trick of the light—but no, there was no explaining it, there was an area of clarity in this large covering of mist.

From the corner of my eye I felt a movement and, as I turned towards it, I noticed a swaying in the orange curtains. They were still closed but I knew that Henry had been watching me and that he too had seen the shape in the oak tree.

I looked back to the high branches—in that instant while I had looked away—the mist had lifted and the whole tree was bright, every leaf clearly visible—but I knew….

I returned to my seat and closed my eyes, picturing it all again. I felt a warmth on my face and knew that the early sun had reached this corner of the town and I sensed the light deep within me had become brighter as if a dimmer switch had moved up once more.

I opened my eyes and focused on the row of houses—all still the same—but wait—there did seem to be something different—some tiny change. I scrutinized this now so familiar scene. What could it be? The curtains were all still closed—the roofs were beginning to dry and steam rose from them as the warmth of the sun touched them.

I sat very still in deep concentration, only my eyes moved—along the row and back, over and over again. It was as if I was doing one of those puzzles in newspapers or children's books—spot the difference—where you had to find the differences in two seemingly identical pictures. I moved all along the row again and then, with a start, I found it. In the paving, outside Mr. Boswell's door, from the tiniest crack, a dandelion had forced its way through and its splendid yellow flower was shining there like a golden sovereign in a muddy street.

In that moment I knew that this was the sign which I had been waiting for. This was the arrow, pointing out my direction. It was centred on this house and its occupant. Somewhere deep inside I had known this all along. This had all been written a long time ago by some unseen hand.

Just then the orange curtains were swept back and I felt Henry's presence and knew he was saying to himself, "About bloody time!"

I had no idea what exactly I had to do but at least I knew where it was to be done—inside this end house—number eight Oak Walk—the place where Mr. Boswell lived.

It would be possible too for Henry to join me again on the bench. He would appear quietly by my side sometime soon.

SIX

It was two days later. I had just finished another healthy lunch and had watched the meals on wheels ladies, come and go—one of the two had faced and survived the delivery to number eight—her turn over for another day. Could it really be so traumatic inside that very ordinary doorway? I asked myself. As I tried to imagine the mysterious occupant of that particular house, Henry made his way towards me, his eyes bright and twinkling. It came as no surprise to me now, that he seemed to know exactly where my thoughts lay.

"Poor old Harry Boswell," he said. "He has shut himself in there. His wife died a year or so ago and he has never got over it . He had lived in her light for so long that when she went, he found himself in a very dark, frightening world. It has made him very afraid, angry and resentful and he scares everyone away. His family have all but given up on him. They did try in the beginning."

I made no comment. I had nothing to say. I waited quietly and soon Henry continued.

"It is a strange thing but a strong light within a person will draw some people around, like moths round a candle flame and it will also cause others to pull away, back into the shadows. You will become aware of this if you haven't already done so. It can be hard to deal with at first but this is just how it is—the ones who go away may return wearing sunglasses, or may in fact stay away." He paused again, then said, almost under his breath, " I cannot help Harry. He has withdrawn too far—it will need a newer, less strong light, to enter his shadow lands...."

Henry was on his way again—he had confirmed what I already knew. Later that day I was to have further confirmation.

During this time I had continued to be a hard working

accountant and my business was as busy as ever. I had a new client booked in at three thirty that afternoon—a Mrs. Elsie Palmer.

I had, over the months, become more aware of my clients as people, rather than merely balance sheets and I studied them closely. I seemed to relate to them in a less formal, less pompous manner.

Mrs. Palmer was a lady in her late fifties, I guessed. She was dressed in her best coat for the occasion. She was obviously uneasy at the prospect of a meeting with an accountant. This was a new experience for her and she seemed nervous and rather agitated. She clutched a bundle of envelopes and leaflets and a large white handbag. There was an umbrella cleverly clipped to the side of the bag. Her hair was neatly styled with what looked like a natural wave and was a fairish brown colour. Her hand, when I shook it, was well worn—a hand that didn't mind hot water and cleaning substances. Her grip was firm and honest. Her face, despite her anxious expression, was open and caring. She was, I could tell at once, a really nice woman.

She sat down on the chair I gestured towards, and declined my offer of tea or coffee, obviously determined to tackle the matters of business without delay.

"I've won a lot of money," she blurted out, her tone inferring that this occurrence was akin to news of a terminal illness. "It's driving me mad. I just don't know what to do about it. I keep worrying and worrying—I'm waking in the night fretting about it. I know it sounds daft—I should be as happy and carefree as anything but I'm not. My doctor said to come and see you. I thought he'd give me a prescription or send me to one of those counsellor people but he seemed to think you were what I needed. So here I am!"

With that she tossed all her papers, bank books, allowance book etc. onto my desk and sat back in her chair. She took a deep breath and laughed. "He was right. I feel better already! A cup of tea would be very acceptable, if it's no trouble."

I ordered the tea and, before I could speak, Mrs. Palmer was off again. "Everybody keeps telling me what to do. They say I'll get put out of my council house because I've got all this money. They say I'll lose my job. They say I shouldn't be taking a job from someone who needs it. But I like my job. What would they all do down at Oak Walk if I just up and left? And I'd miss them, even old Harry Boswell who nobody'll go near. I know he'd miss me even if he never gives me a civil word or as much as a thankyou!" She had run out of breath and I seized my chance.

"Right, Mrs. Palmer," I said trying desperately to take control of the situation, "help yourself to tea—there's milk and sugar on the tray. Let's sort all this out for you. I'll need to ask you one or two questions."

She appeared to be a sensible, level headed capable person but this win on the lottery of several thousand pounds, had really knocked her sideways. However, after I'd taken charge and reassured her that the council would not evict her and her part time job as a home help was safe, she relaxed a bit and listened attentively and answered my questions in a clear and precise manner. When we had gone as far as we could for this visit I asked her more about her work. She was off again … I waited patiently, eager to hear more about her client at number eight.

"Poor Mr. Boswell," she said. She had my undivided attention now. "He can't help himself. It's as if he's forgotten how to be nice. He wasn't always like this. When his wife was alive he was fine—quite pleasant—used to tease me a bit. He and his wife lived in our street then—two down from me. Oh, he kept his garden lovely! You should have seen his roses! They were his pride and joy and that summer when his poor wife was so poorly, he used to cut her a rose every day and take it to her in the hospice. Right from the day she passed away he changed—just seemed to give up. He never worked in the garden again and with the inactivity his arthritis took a grip and he eventually had to move into the sheltered housing in Oak Walk.

They could never get a home-help to stick with him. He was so rude and difficult—had them all in tears, he did. I just ignore his awkwardness. I'm used to it and know he doesn't really mean it, not deep down. It's just his sadness coming out. There is no cheering him up—I've tried my best over the years and got nowhere. I just chat away and though he acts as if I'm a thorn in his flesh, I know he's really glad when I'm there—though to hear the way he speaks to me, you would think I was his worst enemy!

I'd really like to treat him—buy him something with my winnings, but I think he'd probably throw it back in my face—call it charity or the like!"

My intercom buzzed. My next client had arrived.

"Oh I'm so sorry," Mrs. Palmer was on her feet, gathering her bag and her papers together apologising as she did so, "I feel tons better now that you've taken control of all this finance business. I'll think about all you've told me and let you know what I've decided. Sorry for talking on like that—when I get going I don't know when to stop!"

I walked her to the door and said goodbye.

What an incredible woman—and what a coincidence!

Next day as I ate my cheese and pickle sandwich on rye, in my usual place, Henry made himself comfortable beside me. As usual there was no greeting, just a nod and a smile. No waste of time over inane pleasantries regarding the weather, my lunch or the state of the world.

"I believe you met our Mrs. Palmer." Henry said. "She's been singing your praises all morning. According to her, you have saved her from incarceration in a mental institution at the very least!" He chuckled and I grinned.

"She's a very likable lady—I'm glad she felt I'd been of some help." How formal and stuffy I sounded.

It was uncanny the way Henry read my thoughts. No sooner had I recognised my stuffiness than he said, "You need to loosen up, as my grandson would say, or is it lighten up? 'Get a life', is another of his frequent expressions!

Mrs. Palmer certainly has a big heart." Henry continued, " She's the only person who doesn't have a bad word for old Harry, next door. His insults and tantrums just seem to bounce off her. She says they are just his pain being released and are nothing to do with her. She's a very wise woman. I picture her as a sort of Tinkerbelle moving around in that dark house giving out little bursts of light as she tidies and dusts."

And that was my message for the day. Henry was off again. I felt like a long ago Sunday-school child being given his text for the week—words of wisdom to learn from and ponder on.

SEVEN

Two days later, I settled down to study the financial pages of the newspapers—brought in as usual from the front office with my tray of tea and two Abernethy biscuits. As I picked up the pink pages of the Financial Times, a stray piece of paper floated onto the floor. I bent to pick it up, meaning to toss it into the bin.

Over the last months I had begun to notice any unusual occurrences and tried to interpret some meaning into anything different that happened. I was alert to coincidences and synchronicity—so I glanced at this printed page which had slipped past the vigilant eyes and hands of the front office staff.

It had to be significant—I was the great detective searching for leads, for clues. The wizard or soothsayer watching for omens or for signs! I smiled to myself. Was I about to 'lighten up' and 'get a life' as Henry had advised?

The piece of paper in my hand was a white sheet with black printing—a computer made flier. It was headed Library Services, and underneath it said boldly "Books On Wheels". I quickly scanned the sheet. The library service were asking for volunteers to help deliver books once a month to the house-bound in this area.

It all seemed of little consequence but instead of tossing it into the bin beside my desk, I placed it on top of my in-tray and went back to the delights and fascination of my financial pages.

Throughout the day I was conscious of my eyes being directed to that innocuous piece of paper on my in-tray.

Later, as I savoured my afternoon cup of Earl Grey, I reached out for the white leaflet which had winked at me across the desk throughout the day. I fingered it—I scrutinised each word. My mind wandered round and round its content and back again. I could not believe I was even remotely considering becoming a volunteer—a charity worker—a do-gooder!

A mental argument began inside my head and all the reasons why I could not possibly do such a thing were slowly argued down. I could, if I wanted, find the time and why would someone like me not be right for the job? And I had this sort of excited feeling that this might be my way in to number eight Oak Walk.

Why, for a moment, I thought that out of all the house-bound people in the town, I should be sent to the home of Mr. Harry Boswell, I could not imagine. However my newly acquired intuition told me that this was so.

Before I could change my mind, I picked up the telephone and dialled the number printed on this tantalising document.

I explained, to an extremely pleasant young lady, why I was ringing and she asked me to call at the library and talk to their Mr. Mackenzie who was the Housebound Project organiser. He would be on duty that evening until eight. I said I would call in after work and gave my name and telephone number.

The library was a new building set on the edge of the park and near the Council Offices. Nice and central like town planners would wish. I had been here occasionally to make use of the reference part of the library upstairs but I had never been inside the main area. I was not a great reader apart from things to do with work. When I read fiction it was only when on holiday and I bought paperbacks for such occasions, along with sun lotion and mosquito repellent and phrase books!

I decided to take a walk around the vast array of book-laden shelves to get a feel of the books before asking for Mr. MacKenzie. I was amazed as I looked at all the various headings above the shelves—there seemed to be books on every conceivable subject as well as all the works of fiction. And such magnificent books on Art, History, Wildlife, Music, Travel, Cookery, Gardening—the list was endless. Where would a new subscriber begin? I felt like a child let loose in a sweet shop.

I had not belonged to a library since I left home to go to

university. We had had cards then—they were pink I remembered. You handed them over in receipt of the books borrowed and were handed them back on the safe return of the books. I remembered the deft fingers of the librarians as they flicked through the rows of pink tickets and effortlessly produced the correct tickets as if by magic. I could remember, as a small boy, my eyes level with the counter, watching these marvellous fingers with such wonder and admiration.

I looked around and it did seem to be the same sort of system. There was an In desk and an Out desk—people queuing with books at each. I then noticed another desk with a sign on it saying—Enquiries—I headed for that desk—no line-up here—no library person either. Almost immediately, a young girl approached me, smiling helpfully. I told her I wished to speak to Mr. MacKenzie, if he was available.

"He's on the telephone at the moment," she said "but will be free shortly. I'll let you know when he's available."

"Thankyou," I said and before I had realised, I'd asked, "Is this where I get cards for the library books?"

"You want to join?" she smiled. "Well just fill in this card and give it back to me."

I filled in my details and handed it back to her. She went off and returned with one blue card—like a credit card. She told me that I could choose up to ten books with this card and have them for three weeks. There would be a fine to pay if they were not returned by the date stamped on the books. It was possible to renew borrowed books by calling in or in fact by telephoning. And that was that! What a marvellous service! I could, if I wished, walk out of here with ten magnificent books at no cost whatsoever, if I returned them within three weeks. Why, in all these years, had I never made use of this facility? I was mathematically working out in my head how many books I could have borrowed over the last twenty five years, and pondering on this when the young assistant announced that Mr. MacKenzie could see me now. She led me to a table in the far corner.

Mr. MacKenzie was a very serious, bespectacled young man, in his late thirties. He looked very much the archetypal librarian—a meticulous organiser—a fount of all knowledge. The kind of fellow who would be useful on the pub quiz team but not much fun—a bit like an accountant!

I sat down on the chair provided and explained the reason for my visit. He thanked me for coming and reached for the appropriate file—neatly and boldly marked—House-bound Library Services. I was sure that the catchy title of Books on Wheels, was not of Mr. MacKenzie's choosing. He proceeded to tell me all about this service. It had been running for about twelve months and demand was growing all the time.

How it worked was that people who were house-bound, or their carers, applied to the library and were given a form to fill in. At this point Mr. MacKenzie expertly extracted the appropriate form from his file and handed it to me. The information collected on this document would help to identify the type of books preferred. This gave a starting place. As the clients started to select books a profile would be built up. All the information was put into the computer and there was a constant record of which books had been borrowed by each client and they received a new selection each month. They were given a selection of fifteen titles each month and they could choose up to twelve books, which they had for one month. These were then returned when the new selection was delivered the following month. Clients with particular disabilities were catered for—there was the large print selection, and of course the talking books on cassette.

I was very impressed and said so. Mr. MacKenzie continued saying, "Of course we do have to rely very heavily on the help of volunteers, as far as the collect and delivery side of the operation is concerned. Our volunteers have to be car owners and able to carry the baskets of books—this makes them specialised volunteers so to speak. We are having a big advertising exercise, as our numbers have dropped off and we also need relief volunteers to cover, in cases of sickness and holiday leave. New volunteers often like to start off in this way, to see how they like the job. Do you think you might be able to help us with this project, Mr. Fanshaw?"

The librarian looked at me through his tinted lenses with his serious expression—I felt that only the very strong would dare to refuse this man. I felt weak and unsure of myself and stammered, "Well, I don't know if I would be suitable. I've never done anything like this before—I probably could spare an hour or so every month. I work for myself, so I could find the time if I had plenty of notice."

I had answered correctly and Mr. MacKenzie managed a sort of smile, "That's excellent, Mr. Fanshaw, we have a bit of a hole right now—Mrs. Kelsie, she's been a volunteer with us right from the start—a most reliable and charming lady—has to go into hospital next month and won't be available for the next few months. If you could cover for her it would be such a help. She does the sheltered housing delivery, down in Oak Walk. Do you know it?"

Why was I not in the least surprised by this. Deep down I had known that this was where I would be heading.

I affirmed to Mr. MacKenzie that I knew the area and that I would be glad to help.

The librarian got to his feet and extended his hand to me to welcome me aboard. He told me he would arrange for Mrs. Kelsie to ring me to discuss the changeover. He knew she would be relieved that a suitable stand-in had been found. "I'll be in touch," he said, "the week before your delivery date."

I felt like an expectant mother being spoken to by her obstetrician! I thanked Mr. MacKenzie and left the library. I was half way home before I realised that I hadn't chosen any books. Still, I had my card now and could go back any time.

It was three days later, when my home telephone rang. This was quite unusual, I didn't get many calls at home, apart from the occasional salesperson offering double glazing or a new kitchen. A pleasant voice announced that she was Mrs. Kelsie and she'd been given my number by Mr. MacKenzie, at the library. Her voice was low pitched, warm and friendly and there was a hint of an accent—Scottish, I thought.

"I believe you are going to stand in for me with the Books on Wheels service, while I'm out of action," she said .

Yes, that's right," I replied.

She seemed very relaxed yet businesslike and continued, "Would it be possible for us to meet? Then I could fill you in on our clients. It will make the changeover easier for them if you are familiar with their little ways. I'd feel happier too."

I agreed that this would be of help to me and suggested that she call at the office. "It's in the high street—Fanshaw's Accountancy above the video shop." I gave her the address.

"Yes, I know where you mean. How about the day after tomorrow?" I liked her straightforward manner. I quickly checked my diary and affirmed that ten forty five on that day would be suitable.

I was already looking forward to meeting the person behind that interesting voice.

Two days later she was ushered into my office by Fiona. Mrs. Kelsie was an attractive lady—smartly dressed in well fitting brown trousers and a cream top with matching cardigan casually draped over her shoulders. She was of medium height and in her mid to late fifties. She had a ready smile and brown eyes that looked as if they laughed a lot.

I shook her hand—it was warm and dry—a firm hand shake that I liked.

"Tea—Coffee?" I asked holding out a chair.

"Please, a black tea would be lovely." She smiled and sat down.

Mrs. Kelsie opened the folder she was holding. This was a lady who liked orderliness, she was efficient and direct. "Right, I'll fill you in on what you'll be expected to do with these deliveries. I've made notes you can keep, but I'll go over them if you like?" I nodded, quite content to watch and listen.

"You know where Oak Walk is?" she continued. I nodded again. She had no idea just how familiar I was with Oak Walk! "Well we visit four of the houses there. Number one—that's Mr. Paterson. His sight is poor but he can manage the large print, but does have books on tape as well. He loves to talk—mostly about the books he has just read and is returning. He acts as if we've written them all ourselves or at least are closely related to the authors! So he tells you exactly what he liked or didn't like about each one. If he really didn't like a particular author, make a note of it and let Mr. MacKenzie know. Mr. Paterson likes thrillers and espionage stories.

Next door, at number two, is Miss Bryson. She is a very quiet little lady. She probably won't say much. She likes more romantic novels—historical novels and the lighter Catherine Cookson, sort of books. You'll be in and out of this house in no time.

Then at the other end there is Mr. and Mrs. Sinclair, at number six. Mrs. Sinclair is quite frail. She had a stroke and is paralysed on her right side and can't speak very well. Mr. Sinclair is just wonderful with her—totally devoted. He likes westerns, but chooses romances to read to Mrs. Sinclair. We give them a selection of each. They are such a lovely couple. It's a joy to visit them.

Then the last one. I knew what was coming, number eight. "That's Mr. MacFarlane, at number seven," she said. I felt such a feeling of disappointment and disbelief—my face must have shown this, but Mrs. Kelsie was referring to her notes and seemed unaware of my astonishment. "Oh, Mr. MacFarlane—Henry—he is a delight to visit. His house is the same as all the others but it seems to burst with light and brightness even on the dullest days. It is a tonic just to go in there. He likes all kinds of books. He's a bit of a philosopher, I think. He usually has a list of what he wants and often his books are specially ordered. He doesn't have fiction as a rule, but you can never tell with Henry. He is always full of surprises. The other month he asked for 'The Wizard Of Oz' and 'Alice In Wonderland'!

The other houses are fairly predictable but not number seven. It's always a surprise there—always pleasant but always different! I never feel I really know Henry. He makes me think about things. I always seem to leave with a new thought or idea or insight—a new perspective on life. I may not be aware of it at the time but it gradually affects me in some way. I can't describe it. He's a very special man—I know that."

I understood exactly what she meant but said nothing. I knew that someday we would be able to share our thoughts on Henry MacFarlane. I pushed aside my disappointment at the omission of house number eight from my schedule and smiled at Mrs. Kelsie as I said, "thank you so much for this," accepting the folder of carefully constructed notes. "This has been most useful and will be such a help."

She rose to her feet saying, "Do feel free to contact me if you have any queries. I've put my telephone number on the front there." She gestured towards a printed sticker with her name, address and telephone number. "I'd really like to keep in touch with this project. I was in at the start and these clients are my babies, so to speak." She laughed self consciously.

"I'll do my best to baby-sit them for you," I said smiling, as I opened the door for her.

There was a delicate perfume in the office after she left and a lightness in the atmosphere. I sat down, holding the folder between my fingers. What an extremely pleasant woman....!

I felt very relaxed and peaceful after this meeting. Things were going well. I was surprised to find myself looking forward to this voluntary job and actually meeting these people named in the folder and described in such detail by Mrs. Kelsie.

There was only one disappointment—Mr. Boswell was not on the list—his name was not in the folder.

I had been so sure, so certain. I had felt Harry Boswell was the reason I had been directed to do this voluntary work. There had to be a connection. Why else was I delivering library books in Oak Walk?

I began to think about the different books in each person's tray and wondered what sort of books I might select for the unhappy man behind the door of number eight. It was impossible to guess, as I knew so little about the man—in fact I knew nothing at all—not quite—I knew that he used to like his garden and grew beautiful roses. Mrs. Palmer, the home-help, had told me that. I wondered if a beautifully illustrated book on roses might brighten and lighten up the darkness which engulfed Harry Boswell....

EIGHT

The next weeks were extremely busy for me at work and when a call from Mr. MacKenzie was put through to my office, I was quite lost for a moment or two, as he announced importantly that the delivery date for the books was the following week. They were usually delivered on a Wednesday afternoon by Mrs. Kelsie but the day could be altered to suit myself.

I must have sounded rather distracted and distant but a quick glance in my diary showed that, by chance, the next Wednesday afternoon was free of appointments and I arranged to call at the library immediately after lunch.

I was instructed by the efficient Mr. MacKenzie to come to the door at the side of the library and ring the bell. This was the staff entrance. He managed to make this sound like a great honour like attaining the key to the executive toilet!

The weather had been particularly wet recently and I had had no meetings with Henry. I wondered if he would be surprised when he saw who Mrs. Kelsie's replacement was. I had a feeling that he already knew exactly who would carry his tray of books next time.

I was certainly looking forward to my first impressions of the homes in Oak Walk. I only wished that one of these homes had been number eight.

On the following Wednesday, I was surprised to find that I had begun to feel slightly apprehensive and I asked myself several times how I had managed to get myself involved in all of this. What was going on....? Who would have imagined, six months ago, that I would be fitting in time, in my busy schedule, to deliver library books to a group of house-bound pensioners who had absolutely nothing to do with me?

I had to admit that I did not like the feeling of being the new boy and was anxious that I wouldn't make a mess of things on my first day. I was certainly stepping out of my comfort zone and I felt ridiculously vulnerable.

Mr. MacKenzie seemed to loom over me, in my mind, as if he was an authoritative head of chambers and I, a very junior clerk. It brought back memories of similar occasions from my past. That awful sick feeling as I started a new school when I was eight. We had moved to another town and I didn't know anyone and, being an only child, had to cope with this alone.

Then there was the first day at University—the brave cheerful exterior but the jelly legs and churning stomach were there again.

Even my first day as a junior accountant with an excellent degree under my belt, I relived this agonising gripping fear of making a mess of things and looking a fool.

When at last, I had my own business and was of maturing years, I had imagined that this insecurity and apprehensive feeling had gone for ever. These were emotions which I had always hidden and suppressed. I had never, until now, acknowledged them or indeed looked at them. Was this perhaps the reason that such emotions lie dormant and re-emerge, to be experienced again and again in situations like this? Feelings and emotions, which were completely reasonable in an eight year old boy going alone into a new school were now totally inappropriate in a fifty-seven year old professional man about to deliver a few books to some pensioners!

I became aware as I analysed this that I had lived all these years hiding behind a facade of confidence and self assurance. I had never told anyone how I was feeling and no one had ever guessed, as far as I could tell, that deep inside I was anxious and vulnerable and at times very afraid and uncertain.

As this profound revelation hit me I realised that the small boy I had been had been urged into this dishonest pattern of showing the world a false image. He had time and time again been encouraged to be a brave little soldier and hide all traces of fear or distress somewhere deep inside. My parents led by example and never showed their emotions to me or to the outside world. As a result, these and other emotions were pushed down and hidden away under this false veneer. I could see the result of this in the man I had become. A man who showed one face to the public and who wore a mask to hide what was going on inside. This was why I had always had difficulty with close relationships. I was too afraid to take off the mask. I did not know who lived behind it and had this awful dread that no one would like the person underneath. This was the subconscious message I had understood as a child—pretend, pretend, pretend—and the reason for this, I interpreted, was that the real, true me was unlovable and unacceptable!

I took a deep breath and blew it out forcibly like air coming out of a balloon. This was quite a revelation—a real can of worms. These were the sort of issues being dealt with every day by counsellors and psychotherapists, social workers etc. I had been aware of all this being necessary for other, less well adjusted people. I had never for a moment realised that I was in a similar state—my act had been so good and had become so much a part of me that I believed it!

It was one thirty and I was on my way to the library. My confident, professional front well in place. Somehow, now that I knew it was there it didn't seem to fit quite so well—a bit like a sticking plaster which has been loosened to look at the sore beneath and then stuck down again!

I parked the car and walked to the side door and rang the bell as instructed. There was one of these speaker things which asked me who I was in a distorted voice. I have a detestation of talking to machines but gave my name in a disagreeable tone. The buzzer sounded and the door unlocked.

"Ah, Mr. Fanshaw, good to see you." said Mr. MacKenzie when he saw me. "Come this way and I'll show you what's what."

On the table were four red plastic trays, the kind bakers use—each marked clearly with a name and address. This looked idiot proof at any rate. There was a clip board attached to each tray, similarly marked. The attached paper had a list of all the books in the tray and empty columns where I had to mark which books had been selected and the date. There was also a column containing the titles of the books to be returned and space for any comments from the clients. It all seemed simple enough.

"It's quite straight forward. Will you be o.k, Mr. Fanshaw?" Mr. MacKenzie asked.

"Yes, I'm sure I will." I responded and then to my amazement suddenly announced, "I feel quite like the new boy on his first day at school!" When I said this, a visible change took place in the librarian—the stiff formal man opposite seemed to relax and soften.

He actually grinned and said, "I know it can be quite daunting tackling something new—no matter what it is. Mrs. Kelsie's a hard act to follow too. Oh yes, I nearly forgot, if any of them ask after her, tell them she is doing well after her operation and is in Ward 7C at The General."

I suddenly felt part of the team and it felt good. The first hurdle over, I loaded the car and headed for my first assignment—number one Oak Walk and Mr. Paterson.

My apprehensive feeling was now one of excitement and anticipation. I did not feel this was in any way an altruistic, good works sort of thing. I knew this was for my own benefit. This was further education—a widening of my narrow horizons, a step onto a huge learning curve. This was not something I could learn from books—this was what some referred to as the University of Life. I was a new student at this educational establishment—reading feelings and emotions!

I glanced at the trays of books which filled my back and front seats. I wanted to stop the car and explore them all. They looked bright and exciting in their shiny plastic covers. I made up my mind to go into the library and choose books for myself, after I had returned the trays to Mr. MacKenzie.

I parked the car and lifted out the first tray of books and walked the short distance to the house marked number one. I couldn't help glancing up into the oak tree and smiling—'look what you've done to me! Where will it all end?'

I rang the bell, balancing the tray between my body and the door frame. A strong deep voice called out, " It's open—just come in." I pushed the door and stepped into a small hallway. There were three doors—presumably leading to a bedroom, bathroom and sitting room. Two doors were closed and I moved towards the open one, where I was met by Mr. Paterson.

He was tall and slim built and had thinning grey hair. He had a slight stoop. He wore large, very thick glasses and moved very close to me and seemed to scrutinise my face.

He smiled and said, "I heard your car door and was expecting you. I don't normally invite strangers in like that. Just put the tray on the settee. I have the return books there on the table for you."

The room was small but uncluttered—besides the table and two dining chairs, there was a two seater couch and one armchair, a television and a music centre. There was a gas fire with a mantelpiece which held a few photographs and a clock. There was another door leading into what I guessed would be the kitchen. It was all very compact and nicely done.

"How is Mrs. Kelsie? Have you heard?" he asked.

I told him what I knew.

"I've written her a card. Shall I post it or will you be seeing her?" he enquired. Once again I was startled at the words which passed my lips.

"Oh, give it to me. I'd planned to call in at the hospital and take her some flowers." Where had that come from? Until the words were spoken, I had had no such intention. Still it did seem like a good idea.

"I'll leave you to look over these new books and tapes, Mr. Paterson, and I will be back when I've delivered the rest. Will that be o.k.?" I said.

"That'll be fine." He answered, already busy with the new books. He had to hold them up very close in order to read the titles.

I left the house and went back to the car to collect the second tray. So far so good.

Next door—number two, the door was opened before I reached it. Miss Bryson had been watching my progress from her window. I felt she was assessing how the efficient Mrs. Kelsie's replacement was shaping up. Miss Bryson was a tiny lady in every way. Small and birdlike. Everything about her was neat and precise. Her eyes darted about, giving her a nervous, restless appearance.

This house was full of things—ornaments, knick-knacks, memorabilia. On the walls were cross-stitch pictures and there was evidence of other handicraft work—embroidered cloths and antimacassars and a delicate lace table-cloth. There was an immense tapestry work-basket in the corner filled with sewing and knitting materials. I looked at her hands—these were creative tools—these hands were seldom idle. I wondered if somewhere in the house there lurked a cross-stitch quotation of the words—'The devil finds work for idle hands to do?'

This little lady must have been a school teacher. I felt like a school boy in her presence and quite expected to be told to stand up straight, at any moment.

The books for return stood to attention on the table—arranged in alphabetical order, I felt sure. There was a piece of paper beside them—in beautiful hand-writing, each title was listed and underlined with a brief comment made beside each entry. I just knew that this was the kind of reader who would correct any spelling or grammatical errors she came across in the books.

I laid the tray of books down and Miss Bryson, very quickly, made her selection and said, "I shall expect you again, four weeks from today." I was dismissed!

I was half way through my deliveries and had the next tray in my arms and was heading for the Sinclairs at number six. I rang the bell and the door was opened by Mr. Sinclair. He was of medium height, had a bald head and a neat grey moustache. He had a military smartness and posture. He held the door open for me and called out to announce my arrival to his wife. "Yes, Ellie, I was right. It's the man from the library with our books. I said you'd probably be around today. This is my wife, Ellie. She's not been so well. But we manage, don't we? We look out for each other."

A frail little lady with a head of wonderful white curls, sat rather crookedly, in a wheelchair. She leaned to one side and it was obvious that her right arm was paralysed and the right side of her face was slightly affected. She smiled and nodded and managed a decipherable "Good afternoon."

"I'm James Fanshaw—standing in for Mrs. Kelsie." I said rather needlessly but for want of anything better to say. This was all so new to me and I felt out of my depth.

"We do enjoy our books, don't we, Ellie?" Mr. Sinclair continued. "We usually get through two each week. We're still reading this one, so we'll keep it another month. We'll make our new selection when you're in with Mr. MacFarlane next door. That's what we usually do."

"That's fine," I said, "I'll be back shortly."

Now at last, I thought—a familiar face—this would be easier. I swung the last tray out of the car and was on my way into Henry's home.

He was by the open door as I approached—smiling broadly as if he had engineered this whole thing. I couldn't help but laugh back into these dancing blue eyes, magnified behind his large spectacles.

"Well, well—accountant turned delivery boy! How do you like your new job?" I felt I'd known this man all my life. As I stepped into his house—the warmth and brightness met me and it was not just the orange curtains—the lightness seemed to have little to do with the furnishings or paint work—it was all to do with the essence of this man who lived here.

At this time I knew nothing about energies and auras—all I was aware of was that this house—exactly the same as the other three I had been in earlier—was as different as it was possible to be and that difference was all to do with the presence of this old man—this octogenarian who, on the surface, was very ordinary—no outstanding features—nondescript clothes—just a clean, pleasant elderly man with arthritic hips and knees. I was aware that this lightness which emanated from Henry and filled every corner of his home, had entered and filled my being—I felt lighter and brighter and was filled with a warmth and a sort of inner peace.

Henry was watching me—enjoying it all. He, of course, had seen this happen to people, many times before. I did feel that he had some special interest in me and that our lives, for some reason, had become inextricably linked.

"There's tea in the pot, if you fancy a cup," he said. "Mrs. Kelsie usually has one with me if she has the time."

I nodded, "That would be lovely—just as it comes. I have it black."

I sat on the arm of a chair and sipped the tea. Henry was looking at the books. He handled them with reverence and it was obvious that he was particularly delighted by one of the titles. I could feel his excitement and anticipation.

"Good, good," Henry exclaimed, "You've managed to get it for me. I've been waiting ages for this one." He hugged it to his chest and stroked its cover lovingly. I had never seen anyone react with such pleasure to a book. I smiled into Henry's eyes and shared in his joy.

"I've made a note on the books I've read this month." Henry said. And I have listed three titles I would like ordered. Mr. MacKenzie is very good at getting hold of books for me. The library service is marvellous, it really is."

I could tell that Henry's attention was focused on the book he still held tightly and I knew he was eager to be alone with it. In any case I had work to do.

I said goodbye and made for the door, carrying the tray now holding Henry's return books and completed paperwork. On the top lay an envelope. Before I had time to ask if this was meant to go with the books, Henry called out, "Oh that's for Mrs. Kelsie. Give it to her when you see her!" I smiled to myself—as usual he was one step ahead of me!

After placing the tray back in the car, I returned, empty handed to number six. I knocked and entered.

"We're all ready for you now. We've chosen our books and marked up the sheet. Thankyou so much for coming. We'd be lost without our books, wouldn't we, Ellie?" Ellie nodded and gave a lop-sided smile.

"See you both, next month." I smiled back. I couldn't ever remember having felt so appreciated. This feeling was better than any fee. This must be why all those millions of people work in the voluntary sector. I'd never understood it until now.

I was now at my last call—to pick up Mr. Paterson's tray. We greeted each other for the second time and already the strangeness between us had gone. We were no longer strangers—we had met before.

"I had quite a job deciding which books to keep," he said. "They all seemed tempting. Could you mark up the form for me? I enjoyed all the books this time except for that one on the top—I just couldn't get on with the reader's voice—the pseudo American accent got on my nerves and it spoiled what might have been a decent enough story. It's funny how some voices do this. I'm more aware now that my sight is so poor. Some voices seem to lift my spirits right away. I recognise voices at once and don't need to watch the television screen to know what emotions are being expressed. It's wonderful how the other senses are able to compensate for a failing one. Well I mustn't keep you, young man. Thankyou for bringing my books and don't forget to tell Mrs. Kelsie I was asking after her. Tell her I said her replacement is doing just fine—but isn't as pretty!"

We both laughed as I left.

I was back in the car and on my way to the library. I was on a high. What an experience! What an afternoon!

I felt alive and energised—as if a part of me which had been frozen had now melted. I felt sure I must have altered physically—this change could not only be on the inside.

The dimmer switch had turned up again.

Back at the library door, I grinned at the bell with its mechanical voice and with a new lightness of step, I delivered the four trays on to Mr. MacKenzie's desk.

"Well how did it all go?" he asked.

"Fine," I said. "I hope all the paperwork is as it should be."

"I'll show you what I do with it now, if you like? I think it helps if you can see the reasoning behind it all. The whole system will fall into place then."

He moved to the computer and gestured to a chair beside his.

"Each client has a file." He clicked away and on the screen came Mr. Paterson's name and details—followed by lists of book titles, story tapes, dates etc. Mr. MacKenzie held the form I'd completed a few minutes earlier and quickly added all the information I'd been given. The computer now knew to avoid any tapes read by a certain Margerita Dunbar being dispatched to a certain auditorially sensitive Mr. Paterson.

He entered the information from each client in turn. He did a search for the books requested by Henry and put in orders for those not available in the County libraries.

I was most impressed.

"Have you any questions?" he asked.

"No, I don't think so. It has all been most interesting. I must say I have thoroughly enjoyed my afternoon. I'll be glad to help out again next month. Shall I put it in my diary for four weeks today?"

"Thankyou, Mr. Fanshaw. We do appreciate your help. See you in one month."

NINE

I made my way into the main library and looked around—I didn't know where to start. I wandered around in a daze—almost mesmerised. I had no idea what kind of books I wanted to read. How I wished someone would hand me a red plastic tray containing fifteen books to choose from.

I looked around again and began to watch the various people in the library. This was an ideal place for 'people watching'. I had done this over the years while on holiday, in waiting rooms and on trains. I had tried to guess at people's jobs or their relationship to their companions—a sort of game, but frustrating, as there were never any answers. This time was different, I seemed to be looking at these people in a new way—beyond the physical and interpersonal to a deeper more emotional level. I was more interested in trying to gauge how they were feeling—how much joy there was inside them—indeed how bright their energy was. I was soon able to pick out the people who were choosing books for other people—this was a painstaking chore and not a personal pleasure.

What I was hoping to see was someone holding a book the way I had seen Henry holding his, that afternoon. I decided that if I could find such a positive glow around someone, I would choose a book from the same section. It seemed as good a way as any to make my choice. I just hoped I wouldn't be guided to a cookery section by someone who became excited and energised by pictures and descriptions of food!

I moved around watching and waiting. I was studying the borrowers not the books. Then I felt it—I knew that someone, over to my right had made an important discovery—it was as if amidst dozens of people quietly and patiently panning for gold—one had discovered a nugget nestling in the bottom of his pan. No shout—just a drawing in of breath—an excitement, a raising of energy!

I turned slowly—a young woman was engrossed in a book she had newly lifted from a shelf. It was obviously speaking to her. She flicked from one part to another and was clearly delighted with what it contained. She closed it, picked up her bag and holding her find with that reverence Henry had had for his book, made her way to the Out counter. She had decided that this one book would satisfy her. She needed no other that day.

Right, I would stick to my plan and choose from the same section. I just hoped it was not the section devoted to embroidery or quilting!

The section, to my relief, was headed—Philosophy—well that was a wide subject at least. I decided I would choose three books to start with. The first book I pulled from the shelf was about meditation. I would give that a try. The second book was about colour and its affect on body, mind and spirit. That sounded promising—orange curtains springing to mind. My third and final choice was a small insignificant book wedged at the end of a row. As I read its title I caught my breath in amazement. It was called, Seeing Energy Feeling Light. This was today's golden nugget!

I located my brand new library card and joined the queue at the Out Desk. I was so excited. I felt that anyone 'people watching' would wonder what had caused this sudden skip in my step and light in my eyes.

I am sure, when I returned to the office, in such high spirits after a two hour disappearance, the girls wondered what sort of clandestine meeting I'd been attending. They would not have believed that my happy enlivened demeanour had been brought about by simply delivering library books to the elderly house-bound in Oak Walk and selecting for myself, three library books. I am positive that they imagined a much more startling and lurid scenario.

I suddenly remembered that I had agreed to yet another commitment that afternoon. My hand moved to my jacket pocket and pulled out the envelopes which I had promised to deliver to

Mrs. Kelsie. I couldn't believe I had volunteered to do this. How nonchalantly the words had slipped from my lips, "Oh yes, I'll be visiting her. I thought I would take her some flowers!" It is always an unsettling experience to hear words coming from your own mouth in your own voice, that seemed to have by-passed your brain. It seemed to be happening to me more and more these days. Still, when I thought about it, it would be a nice gesture. It was a good idea. I felt like saying, "I wish I'd thought of that!"

I buzzed to the front office and spoke to Julia, "Would you mind nipping out to the florists before you finish. Get me some flowers—nothing too elaborate—and ring the General and find out when visiting is tonight—Ward 7C."

More fuel for their fertile imaginations, I thought.

What a peculiar day this had been and it still wasn't over. I was now on my way into the hospital car park, a large bunch of flowers on the seat beside me. I was beginning to have grave doubts about the wisdom of this visit. How would Mrs. Kelsie feel about a practical stranger walking in to see her in Women's Surgical? Perhaps it would be best if I just left the flowers and the cards and my good wishes at the desk at the end of the ward. With this new plan of action decided, I asked the nurse on duty for Mrs. Kelsie—holding out the flowers and cards.

"Oh, she'll be delighted with these—she's got no visitors tonight. Go right in—its the fifth bed on the right."

I had no choice, I had to stride forth. I stopped at the end of the fifth bed. Mrs. Kelsie, was sitting in a chair, beside the bed, dressed in a most becoming dressing gown in a deep blue colour. She laid aside the book she had been reading and smilingly said, "Mr. Fanshaw! What a lovely surprise. How good of you to come, and what beautiful flowers too!"

I smiled back and held out the envelopes—"You are missed on Oak Walk—These are for you."

She really was a lovely lady—she put me at my ease right away. She made me feel as if we were old friends. She wanted to know all about my book deliveries and smiled as I described each visit. We chatted with an ease and fluidity that I had seldom experienced before and when the bell rang to announce the end of visiting, I was surprised that so much time had passed. We shook hands and both knew we would be in touch again before too long.

I mention this day in great detail as it was so full of changes and new experiences for me. However in the weeks prior to this and in the months following, many small occurrences were forced into my awareness. Small incidences, remarks, words I'd overhear or read—feelings I'd have, memories long forgotten recalled—all of little consequence on their own but when added together, they were quite remarkable. It was a wonderful slow dawning of awareness and with it came an overpowering thirst to know more.

I devoured these first three books with the passion of a man deprived of food for many weeks. I did in fact feel a bit like a hostage who had been released from prison after having been held in captivity for a long time. I was savouring every experience, seeing everything, as if for the first time—determined not to miss a single sensation.

I did not speak of all this for a long time. It was too precious to me and indeed I did not have the words with which to describe it. However people like Henry and Mrs. Kelsie, seemed to know already and they would smile knowingly as they watched my excitement over each new discovery. They knew because they too had experienced it.

Over these months I began to meditate and listen deeply to the stillness. I began to trust my instincts and be awake to the signs of direction going on around me.

I was aware of feeling more alive and in tune with the people and the things in my life. I became more positive in outlook and less judgemental and critical. I mellowed and was gentler and kinder to others and to myself. And the extraordinary thing was that people and things seemed to be kinder and gentler with me.

I often wondered if acquaintances and neighbours thought I was taking some new medication or illegal drugs or had found religion. I suspect though that most of them would be quite unaware of any change in me at all. Certainly the man I used to be would not have noticed a thing, closeted inside his shell of safety and isolation.

TEN

In the four weeks between my library duties I had not forgotten the house at the end of Oak Walk and Harry Boswell. I was still awaiting guidance and direction regarding this.

    I had spent a lot of time on the bench under the oak tree—sometimes alone and sometimes companionably with Henry. He listened patiently as I talked about the books I was reading—bubbling over with the enthusiasm of a new recruit. He would make the odd pertinent comment—putting a complex idea into the simplest of interpretations. It was as if he had a marker pen and was able to highlight the significant points for me. I valued this greatly. He did not lead me in any direction but seemed to be able to let me know when I had discovered the way for myself. It was as if he said, 'yes, now you've got it—now move on!' He was not my teacher, nor my mentor, nor my guide—he was more my loyal supporter—the hand on my back—full of encouragement—quiet enthusiasm—urging me forward. If I asked him a direct question, he usually turned it back to me slightly rephrased, or made some almost unconnected comment, which changed my train of thought and brought me an answer. He was of course, using the best teaching method there is.

One day, as I sat alone on the bench, Mrs. Palmer came bustling along, pulling a laden shopping trolley at her heels. She called across to me a cheery good morning and came to join me.

    "It's a lovely spot you've found here, Mr. Fanshaw. I wish the old folk would come out and sit here more often. I'm sure it would make them feel better. I hear you are standing in for Mrs. Kelsie with the library books. I've been hearing all about you from my old dears. They've taken quite a shine to you by all accounts. I told them how you had rescued me from the brink of insanity!" Her eyes fell on the end house—number eight, and she sighed, "He's no better. I wish there was something you could do for him. He's the most miserable thing you ever saw.

That house is so dark and depressed—I clean and polish it but it doesn't get any brighter. Hardly anyone ever goes into that house and, if they have to, they stay as short a time as possible." She paused, as if at a loss, then said, "I wonder if you could take him some library books. I doubt if he'd look at them—but you just never know. He does read his newspaper and devours every gloomy depressing item—same with the news on the telly—he only hears the bad bits. Like attracts like you could say! What do you think, Mr. Fanshaw?"

The seed had been planted.

"I'll ask at the library, if you like, see if we could just have a tray of books for Mr. Boswell—leave a tray of books with him for a week or so and see what happens! You tell Mr. Boswell, that I'll call next Wednesday afternoon!"

"Right I'll do that. But you'd better be prepared for rudeness and abuse. He's got no time for interfering do-gooders. I just let it all wash over me and keep smiling. Well I'd better get on—he'll be moaning that I've been time wasting again." The home-help laughed and was on her way—shopping trolley in tow.

I didn't know if I had promised the impossible, but this seemed a way forward—a means of entry to number eight Oak Walk and a face to face meeting with the infamous Mr. Harry Boswell.

I decided that if Mr. MacKenzie would not allow me a tray of books, because Harry was not registered on the system, I could surely borrow books for him, on my card.

I had a good feeling about this plan and was impatient to implement it as soon as possible. I had to be prepared that Harry might reject the books totally, but I had an instinct that they would get his attention one way or another. I did not think that he would be able to resist, at least having a peek to see what titles had been chosen for him—even if it was just to allow him to complain about them. I felt sure that if they were left lying in his front room for a month he would, at the very least, look at the titles.

As soon as I was back at my desk, I put a call through to Mr. Mackenzie at the library. I could tell that he was surprised to hear from me so soon and I got the feeling that he thought I was about to pull out of his volunteers' rota. I could hear the relief in his voice when he realised that this was not the reason for my call.

I explained about Mr. Boswell and what I wanted to arrange. I think the librarian felt I was taking this voluntary job a bit too seriously, and perhaps was in danger of over stepping the unwritten job description! Still he agreed my idea was worth trying but said that he could not hand out books without a request from Mr. Boswell. This was not the way the scheme had been set up. He did agree that if the books were issued on my card—and were therefore, my ultimate responsibility—he could not object. If Mr. Boswell liked the books, he could then apply to become an official subscriber to the Books On Wheels scheme.

I had rather expected this response. I knew Mr. MacKenzie would be a stickler for red tape and rules and regulations. Still the plan could go ahead next month. Harry would never know that he was having special treatment. He would have a red tray of books, just like the others—ten books instead of fifteen and no selection required—not on his part at least!

Over the next few days, I kept wondering about the types of books I would select for Harry's tray. One on roses was a definite choice. I knew that Fiona's Bert was a keen greyhound man and I asked her, one day, if this was a family interest. She laughed and told me that her father-in-law could not stand dogs of any kind, though she did know that Bert's grandfather had had a dog up until going into sheltered housing, "They don't allow pets in there" she said, looking sad. "It must be awful to be forced to give up your pet just because you are old. It just isn't right."

I felt my eyes fill with tears and turned away quickly. In that moment I connected with Harry—losing his dog must have been the last straw for him, having lost his wife, his home, his garden and then his dog. I felt his pain and his despair. Would a book about dogs be the last thing he would want to see? I wasn't sure.

I spent an hour one evening just wandering around the library shelves—trying to make my choice for Harry Boswell. I was working almost entirely on guess work with a little of my newly acquired intuitive skills.

This was a bit like the long running radio programme—Desert Island Discs—except I was choosing books instead of records and they were for somebody other than myself.

New ideas kept coming into my head when I least expected—in the middle of the night—while showering—even during a meeting with a client. I made a mental note of every suggestion.

In the end, I chose two fictional books—one about a prisoner of war camp, nice and depressing— to suit Harry's state of mind, and a science fiction escapist novel, and also The Incredible Journey, to bring in an animal interest. Then there was the beautifully illustrated book on roses—Harry, I was convinced, would be unable to resist this. I chose another gardening book about country gardens. I put in a book about classic cars and motorcycles and two travel type books, one within the United Kingdom, the other more exotic places. I had no idea if Harry had any interest in sport, so played it safe and put in a book by an Olympic sportsman—an autobiography. I had one more to choose and, on an impulse, popped into the tray the book about colour which I had had in my first selection.

Mr. MacKenzie had lent me a plastic tray like all the others and I noticed his eyes run over the titles I had chosen, in what I felt to be a rather condescending manner. I felt he was thinking a trained librarian would have made a different selection. I asked if it would be all right if I left the tray with Mr. Boswell on this special delivery, as I wanted to arrange the books in a specific way so that I would be able to tell if they had been moved. Mr. MacKenzie, by now, had decided I was in the midst of some mid-life crisis. He nodded and went back to his computer screen. He wanted nothing more to do with my games and intrigues. I duly moved the books into a disorderly arrangement—some books back to front, others upside down, and made a note of each title and the position of each book with regard to its neighbour. I would inform Mrs. Palmer that on no account was she to touch the books and, provided that no other caller touched them, (I could do nothing to control this) we would know if Harry had handled them. This, I realised, was not a very scientific test but it was all I could think of.

I made the deliveries to my regular four houses and found I was welcomed as a regular caller now and no longer the new boy. I was impatient to get this part over. My mind was totally focused on the last call of the afternoon and my meeting with Harry Boswell at number eight.

Henry, of course, without being told, knew all about it and didn't even bother offering me tea. He, I think, was enjoying my discomfiture a little, and I knew he would be watching my exit from next door with considerable fascination. He would be able to guess from my demeanour how Harry had affected me. He would be able to see if I had been dulled by my sojourn in that dark place.

I felt full of trepidation as I walked towards the green door. I did not know what to expect but I knew that, if my approach was wrong, I would be leaving very rapidly, with the tray of books still in my arms. I was aware that this might be my one and only chance with Harry Boswell.

I wedged the plastic tray against my side and knocked on the door. I knew that Henry was urging me on and wishing me luck. A voice deep and monotonous, called out, "The door's not locked—come in if you must!"

I was horrified to hear my voice—the dreaded bright and cheerful tone and banal words of the stereotypical do-gooder, lady bountiful, religious enthusiast. I wouldn't have been at all surprised if I'd said, 'Well, and how are we today then?' What I did say was not much better and probably sounded just as annoying to the elderly man hunched in a well worn arm chair next to a dull gas fire.

" I'm Mr. Fanshaw, a volunteer from the library. I've brought you some books. Did Mrs. Palmer tell you I would be calling?"

"Oh yes, she did and I told her what you could do with your bloody books! I don't want any of your do-gooding charity. Why can't people mind their own business and stop sticking their noses in where it doesn't concern them! Haven't I enough to put up with without the likes of you—volunteers—social workers—home helps and the like. Never a moments peace, I can tell you. How would you like trails of people in and out your home every day, shoving food, cleaning, laundry services, outings, religion, whatever, at you, and now you want to clutter up my house with piles of stupid books!"

He stopped at last—waiting and watching out of the sides of his eyes, for my reaction. He was almost enjoying this I thought. I stood back shell-shocked, as this tirade was launched at me. Fortunately, he didn't give me time to make any response.

As he continued to vent his fury over my unwelcome intrusion, I took the opportunity to look round the room. It was not as I expected. Dull it was—dark it was—miserable and sad, but this had nothing to do with the furnishings. Apart from the old arm-chair, which had seen better days, the furniture was beautiful—genuine antique I was sure—a mahogany sideboard—too large for the small room, but nicely carved and highly polished, no doubt thanks to the unappreciated Mrs. Palmer. There was an extremely handsome grandfather clock and the television rested on a fine mahogany writing table. There were two other chairs—carver dining chairs with red and gold covered seats and a drop leaf table set against the left hand wall. This furniture had, at one time, been loved and cherished but now, despite the polish, it was lacklustre, sad and unappreciated.

I suddenly realised that Harry had stopped talking again and was staring at me, awaiting my reaction.

"Well?" he said, waiting to hear expected platitudes and smarmy words from me.

Whoever was in charge of my voice, had changed tack and I heard myself say in a strong voice, "I'm not here to do you any favours, Mr. Boswell, I'm just asking you to help me out. But if you can't be bothered, I'll be on my way." I picked up the tray of books which I had rested on the table....

The old man had not expected this and said, "Wait a minute. What are you on about. There's no need to take that attitude. What is it all about?"

"We are trying to extend the Housebound Library service." I answered, "If we don't get a few more subscribers the project may have to fold" I lied with authority. "All I want is to leave this tray of books here for a week or so. You'd be helping to keep the service going for the others. But if it's too much of an inconvenience, I'll take them away with me and try one of the others in the row."

To my great relief, Harry said, "You may as well leave them—I won't be reading any, mind you. Shove them over in that corner so I won't be falling over them." He gestured to the end of the sideboard, near the window. "I'll let you store them here. That home - help woman will just go on and on at me if I don't. She could nag for Britain, that one. Never shuts up, I can tell you! Right then—You'd better go—I've got things to do!"

That was it. With a thank you I was closing the door—mission accomplished—the bait in place!

It was hard to know how I felt at that moment. I could not face Mr. MacKenzie right then. I needed time by myself. I had a great need to sit quietly somewhere and just be with this experience. I drove down to the canal and left the car and walked along the tow path. It was peaceful here. I found a bench and sat there awhile. I realised I had taken on some of Harry's despair. I felt engulfed in his sadness and his pain. I needed to feel this and as long as I knew these were not my feelings this was all right. I'd merely borrowed them for a while, to look at them and learn from them—a bit like the library books!

This man, who so concerned me, had built a shell of emotions around himself—a huge thick wall of anger, grief, irritability and bloody-mindedness. He had subconsciously decided that anything he became fond of would be taken away—his wife, his dog, his garden had already gone and he was not about to become fond of anything ever again. It was too painful.

At this moment I really understood Harry Boswell and I wept inside for him and perhaps for myself too as I realised, that in a way, he mirrored a part of me. To a lesser degree, I too had erected unseen barriers—a protective veneer against disappointment, disapproval and rejection.

This was to be no easy task. I was going to have to chip away at Harry's wall of protection—avoiding any flack flying towards me. If I couldn't get in one way, I would have to find another entrance. I knew that deep in the centre, behind the layers, there was a light still there. It was turned down very low—just as it had been with Henry. I couldn't reach the dimmer switch as yet, but I knew with a certainty that some day I would reach that switch and the first glimmer of light would re-emerge—a match struck inside a dark black hole.

As I focused on this I felt the gloom lift from my shoulders and I felt ready to return to civilisation and Mr. MacKenzie at the library.

There was nothing more I could do for the time being. I had to be patient and wait to see what happened next, behind the dark curtains at number eight. Would a glimmer of light appear or would the books lie untouched, gathering dust, until Mrs. Palmer flicked over them with her busy duster each week.

I had spoken to Mrs. Palmer after I had deposited the books in Harry's front room. We had agreed that this was our secret and no one need know what we had planned. I gave her a copy of the layout of the books and she would check, on each visit, to see if any books had been moved. She said in a conspiratorial tone that she would keep me informed. We were like a couple of undercover cops or secret service agents. A more unlikely duo would have been hard to imagine!

ELEVEN

I was sitting on the bench with Henry one day, two weeks later, feeling a bit fed up at the seeming lack of progress, when Harry's door opened and Mrs. Palmer came to the doorway and shook a yellow duster vigorously—at the same time, making a huge nod in my direction and the most blatant wink. I must have winced at her lack of subtlety but I felt such an excitement, as if I was an angler and my line had tightened for the first time. Beside me, Henry chuckled with delight as I tried to cover up what had occurred. He, of course, as always, knew exactly what was going on and was enjoying every minute of it.

"I do believe a drop of dust has escaped the duster of the scrupulous Mrs.Palmer and has landed on Harry's dimmer switch." Henry said as he moved away slowly, still chuckling to himself.

I remained on the bench, awaiting the accidental meeting with the home-help, as she headed for the shops.

As she approached me I could see she was about to burst with excitement, and I could feel it too. She took up a position beside me—a sort of 'fancy meeting you here' sort of stance and, in her best espionage whisper said, "The rose book has been moved! It was back in the same place in the tray but was turned the other way. He's definitely looked at it!"

She was off again—a jaunty wave and a tug on her shopping trolley and not a backward glance.

How often, during these months, I smiled at the twist my life had taken—from being a rather staid accountant I had become a home-help's accomplice and a book deliverer's stand in!

I had kept in touch with Mrs. Kelsie since the hospital visit. She had dropped me a note, beautifully hand written, thanking me for my flowers and my visit. She said she was now home convalescing and she invited me to call in and up-date her on our shared library work.

I visited Mrs. Kelsie, a day or so after I'd made my second delivery of books. We chatted like old friends and I learned more about the lives of the residents in Oak Walk. She, of course, had heard about the bad-tempered recluse at number eight—everyone knew about him. At least, they all knew his bad points, recounted at length, by all the various volunteers and workers who came and went in the residences of sheltered housing. The pensioners had had to comfort a stream of home-helps who had been assigned to Harry Boswell, prior to the arrival of Mrs. Palmer. They had been regaled by tales of his rudeness to the kindly Meals-on-Wheels ladies and then there were the Bob-a-Job scouts and the Carol Singers. Even the long suffering Jehovah's Witnesses had stopped calling at number eight!

Mrs. Kelsie went on to say, how relieved she had been that Harry Boswell had not asked for library books. When she said this, I felt I had to confess to her what I had done. It was her patch after all.

Before I knew it, I was telling her the entire story. I was horrified to hear myself opening up so thoroughly to this woman I had known for such a short time. Never in my entire life, had I spoken about myself in this way. I had only meant to tell her about the books which I'd left with Mr. Boswell but somehow, I went back to the beginning, and what happened under the oak tree and all the coincidences, the signs and of course all about Henry and the orange curtains.

When I eventually went quiet, I hardly dared to look at the lady opposite. I wanted to get up and run away. I felt naked and vulnerable, a bit like a child who has made an embarrassing scene in public.

"How wonderful!" she said, "how absolutely wonderful!" She got up and walked to her bookcase. She reached up to the top shelf and pulled down a book, "Have you read this?" she asked, handing it to me.

"The Celestine Prophecy," I read the title aloud, "No I haven't read it."

"You must. Take it with you. I know you'll enjoy it and I want to know what you think of it. I am starting to go out again. Let's meet up for coffee next week—The Top Lock Tea Rooms, by the canal. We'll be able to sit outside if its fine. Would Sunday week at two, suit you?"

It was agreed and I got up to leave clutching the book she had leant me. How well she had handled my discomfort and I felt that this book was somehow going to say to me, what she had felt she wanted to say to me.

That evening, I read the book from start to finish. I sat well into the night and literally didn't put it down. I felt myself nodding as I read the story—this book had, I felt sure, been written just for me and had been placed in my hands at just the right moment, when I was ready to read it.

TWELVE

When I looked back over the previous six months, I could see a pattern, a plan, an unfolding of events. The turning on of my awareness that first morning had been the key to all that followed. I knew then, with a certainty, that there was, out there somewhere, a vast power—an energy centre—call it what you will—a resource, waiting to be used. It was available to all, but you had to know it was there before you could begin to use it.

This enlightenment—because that is exactly what it was—had come to me gradually—little messages—insights and discoveries. It had to be this way—no one could teach you. You had to be ready to begin the journey and, once you had stepped on to this magical path of awareness, the lessons and the teachers would appear—stepping in and out of your life—nudging, signaling, hinting, sometimes kicking, screaming and gnawing away, until each penny dropped and a further enlightenment dawned.

This was what Henry had talked about—his on-going illumination—a light becoming brighter and brighter, preparing the way for the final step into the ultimate brightness.

I knew, in this moment, that I had begun a new part of my life—a big adventure—a journey of discovery that would give a direction and purpose to my life. I had found a reason for being here. I was an explorer in search of enlightenment. I had taken my first, hesitant steps. It was exciting and challenging. I had no idea what lay ahead but I no longer felt alone. There were now friends and teachers waiting to be met. They were everywhere.

The most inconsequential occurrence could be the next arrow pointing the way. One book I had read said 'listen to the whispers' and this was exactly what it was all about. That screwed up piece of paper which missed the rubbish bin and slipped under the desk, and remained there for months, might hold a revelation, an insight, for the person who eventually discovered it.

When I realised that nothing is ever insignificant I was filled with a new wonder in the world around me. The simplest, the most mundane—the dreariest moment could hold an insight of the most enriching kind.

I had had a call from Mrs. Palmer the following week to inform me that the rose book had moved again and that the cottage garden book had also been out of the tray and replaced in a different position. With this knowledge, I returned to collect the tray of books from number eight Oak Walk.

I had decided to collect Harry's tray a week before the others. For one reason, my card only allowed a three week loan and also I felt it would be a good idea to leave Harry without books for a week. I felt sure he would miss their presence.

With a deep breath and an imaginary protective shield around me, I knocked and entered Harry's house once more. Everything, including the occupant, seemed exactly as before—still dark and heavy and sad. I gave no cheery greeting, just a polite, business-like good afternoon. I was given a sort of bad-tempered grunt in reply. Harry managed to convey that he had been rudely interrupted and that he was being distracted from some very important task—yet he was sitting there in the old arm-chair with nothing at all going on. The television was switched on but I felt that it was just moving pictures and background noise.

I moved over to the tray of books. They were like old friends, having been in my thoughts such a lot, over the weeks.

"Have you found these a nuisance, Mr. Boswell?" I asked.

"I never went near them," he said and I knew he was lying. He wasn't very good at it. "It's not exactly a thing of beauty, lying there is it? Cluttering up my room!" he complained.

"Well thank you for helping me out" I said. "If it is in your way and you're not at all interested in the library service, I can see if one of your neighbours might accommodate my tray next time!"

As I said this I could tell this was not going the way he wanted. He moved uncomfortably in his chair and remarked, "Oh don't bother—I'll help you out again. I hardly notice them over in that corner."

"That's very kind of you" I said. I produced my list of books—"I know you haven't looked at the books but could I just make a note of the titles here and if they might or might not have been of interest to you?"

"I suppose so, if it won't take too long" he grunted.

"Do you mind if I turn the television down for a moment?" I dared. He glared at me, but complied. I just want you to rate each book on a scale of one to ten—ten being the most interesting. I do know you are not at all interested in any of them but just give me some numbers to satisfy them at the library." I said encouragingly. I lifted up each book in turn and said what kind of book it was. He grudgingly and with seemingly little thought, gave me numbers in the range of one to three. He was determined to show no enthusiasm, but there was an apparent degree of honesty as he gave the two gardening books scores of three. He had cooperated better than I had dared hope and I chanced my luck and said, "Is there a kind of book you would have preferred in the selection?" At once I realised I had made a grave mistake. The word preferred, seemed to annoy him—it seemed to infer that he was involved in this nonsense. He was furious and shouted,

"I told you, I'm not interested in your stupid books. I never asked for any books. I'm only giving them house room as a favour to you and that home-help busybody. Shove anything you like in your stupid tray—it'll make no difference to me!"

"Right" I said, "Thank you again for helping me out. I'll bring a new selection next Wednesday."

Harry turned the volume on the television to full volume and totally ignored the hurried departure of me and the books.

I knew he was sorry to see at least two of the books leave his room and I knew he would be waiting with anticipation, the arrival of the next tray of books from the library. He had been clever enough to make sure that I had scores of three against the type of books he wanted again. He had rattled the numbers off at me, as if at random, but he had been cunning enough to get his message across. I smiled to myself as I walked back to the car. I had a growing admiration for the man hiding behind the mask, and I felt he too had a sneaking respect for me. We both knew, deep down, what the other was up to. We were like chess players locked in battle.

The Sunday following this encounter was the day I had arranged to meet Mrs. Kelsie. I had read her book again, this time at a slower pace and I was eager to discuss it with her. I would also be able to update her on the Harry Boswell saga and perhaps get her help with suggestions on what to try next.

I was looking forward to our meeting. I seemed to be looking forward to and enjoying lots of things these days. I felt more alive and more involved in life than I had ever been before.

It was a beautiful late summer afternoon as I walked along the path beside the canal, heading for the tea rooms. I was like an excited child going to a party. I felt the small child inside me give a whoop and a skip of delighted anticipation. This felt so real that I hurriedly looked over my shoulder just in case I had, in reality, acted out this carefree feeling. Thankfully no one was giving me a second glance. It had just been an extremely vivid imagining. 'Thank Heaven for that' I smiled to myself. What would the town have made of the sensible accountant, skipping and whooping along the tow path on a quiet Sunday afternoon!

I was still laughing to myself as I approached the tea rooms. Mrs. Kelsie, in a charming, deep blue summer suit, was waving to me from a table close to the canal. I made my way to join her. As I sat down, she said, "I could see you were laughing to yourself as you arrived. What was it that you found so amusing?"

I wasn't quite so surprised this time, when I found myself sharing my thoughts and feelings with her. This lady had this affect on me.

"The strange thing is" I concluded, "I was never, as far as I can recall, a skipping, whooping kind of child."

"Perhaps you always wanted to be and repressed it for some reason?" she smiled.

"That could well have been true." I said, almost under my

breath. This thought saddened me.

The waitress arrived and we ordered tea, scones and cakes. It all felt very natural, as if we had done this sort of thing many times before.

"I don't even know your name," I said, "it seems ridiculous, I feel as if we've known each other for ages. I'm James." I held out my hand in a mock gesture. She put her hand in mine and said,

"I'm Frances. It's good to meet you, James!" She laughed with her eyes.

The tea arrived just then and that took our attention for a few moments.

I had laid her book on the table when I arrived. I picked it up and handed it to her remarking, "You were right. I did enjoy it. I've read it twice, would you believe? The first time—the night you lent it to me, I read it straight through at one sitting. The second time, I read it more slowly. I felt it had been written just for me."

She nodded, "I know what you mean. Some books do that, don't they?"

We chatted companionably and it was good to be able to talk to her about what had happened regarding the library books and Harry Boswell. She could sense how I felt about him and wanted to help. We talked about possible titles with which to tempt him. But we were both stabbing in the dark.

It was nearly four o'clock when she looked at her watch and hurriedly got to her feet saying, "Oh is that really the time? I have someone visiting me at five. I must go. Sorry to rush off like this." She held out her hand and as she did so, a tiny gold star fell onto the white linen table cloth. I picked it up on the tip of my finger and looked at it.

"Wherever did this come from?" I remarked.

"Oh that's from me," she laughed. "They get everywhere. My niece in America always puts them inside her cards and letters when she writes. They are called Sprinkles or something like that. I keep finding them everywhere—they appear all over the house. Sometimes she sends tiny coloured hearts, another time it was gold and silver angels! It has been lovely—we'll meet again soon. Sorry to dash off!" she said as she left.

She was gone, leaving behind, an empty chair, a hint of perfume and a tiny gold star!

I kept the gold star—holding it tightly between my thumb and forefinger, as I made my way slowly back home.

THIRTEEN

I was very busy at work the next week and had little time to dwell on the forthcoming delivery of books to Harry Boswell. By the Wednesday, I still had no idea what books to give to the lonely old man at number eight. I decided I would just choose books at random, when I went to collect the regular trays for delivery. This, I thought, would be as good a way as any.

I hurried to the library, skipping lunch, and made a rather rapid selection. I knew Harry would probably ignore most of the titles. I found another book on roses—old fashioned varieties—a lovely book on container gardens, and as an afterthought, slipped in one all about house plants. I added a book on tropical fish—a murder mystery, a book about Winston Churchill, a history of Windsor Castle, a biography about a former England cricket captain, and a western. I decided that the tenth book would be from the philosophy section. As I approached this more familiar area of the library my eyes were drawn to something glinting on the carpeted floor. I stooped down and to my surprise found another tiny gold star. Had this, I wondered, fallen from Frances' sleeve or from a book she'd been reading?

An idea was growing in my mind—if I put different 'sprinkles'—was that what Frances had called them—inside the pages of Harry's books, I would be able to tell if he had opened them. Mrs. Palmer would find them as she cleaned! I would give this some thought before the following delivery date.

I scanned the titles lined along the shelves, hurriedly, seeking inspiration, and there it was—a dark covered book with tiny stars dotted all over it—they looked like spots until you looked closely. It was called 'A Million Lights In The Darkness' and when I read the resume, on the back cover, it was about the author's battle with loneliness and grief. I gathered it up with the rest of the books. I'd read it even if Harry did not. I picked the gold star from the carpet and placed it between the pages of this last book—pages fifty eight and fifty nine—I noted this down as well as the lay-out of the books on the tray.

This was my third library delivery to Oak Walk and I was enjoying the experience more each time and really looked forward to my brief visits at each house. They had all relaxed with me, even Miss Bryson seemed less critical and less suspicious of me—she still intimidated me a little—and I felt in the presence of an old-fashioned schoolmarm who liked clear diction, good posture, and no nonsense!

Mr. Paterson seemed to enjoy my visits. He coped so well with his failing eyesight. He liked to go into great detail, as he recounted the story lines of his talking books, as he referred to them. He had a wonderful ability to describe the voices on the tapes and could mimic accents to perfection. He had a marvellous sense of humour and a great memory. He always told me a new joke before I left, so I was usually chuckling to myself as I left his home.

The Sinclairs always made me feel most welcome. They liked to tell me the gossip—he spoke and she nodded, managing the occasional words, to remind him what story he was to tell me about the latest goings on in Oak Walk. The various callers kept the residents in touch with all that was occurring in the neighbourhood.

That afternoon, Mrs. Sinclair gestured to her husband and pointed to the books, struggling to say something—it sounded like Bosnia. We were both at a loss and she became quite agitated and kept saying the word over and over again. Mr. Sinclair looked perplexed at first then, with relief, a dawning appeared on his anxious face and he said, "Yes, yes, I've got it, Dear. You want me to tell Mr. Fanshaw about Mr. Boswell and the books?" Mrs. Sinclair relaxed and nodded.

I looked surprised. How did they know about Harry's books? Had Mrs. Palmer been speaking out of turn?

Mr. Sinclair explained, "We had a new social worker here last week. A young lass—long dark hair with these bead things in and a pierced nose.

What was she called? A very odd name—Mercedes—that was it. We laughed about that, I can tell you! Well, she came in to us in a right old state. They usually are after they've been in at number eight. We usually have to give them tea and sympathy. This girl was almost in tears.

She'd had the usual bad mouthing from Harry Boswell. He's usually particularly awkward with the new, younger ones. She said she'd walked over in his room and lifted up a book. Well, he went mad at her and told her in no uncertain terms, not to touch these books—he was minding them for Mr. Fanshaw, from the library, and they were for him and no one else was meant to touch them and she'd better get her snooping, interfering, do-gooding backside out of his place before she did any damage.

We didn't know Harry Boswell took library books. Anyway we thought you'd like to know he is taking such good care of them. Like a rottweiller, the way he was protecting them, Mercedes said."

We all laughed.

I was glad to escape and moved thankfully to Henry's house and a welcome cup of tea. He, no doubt, knew all about Mercedes and Harry, but he did not mention it.

Our conversation was about his books and the new ones he was hoping to borrow from the library. He said he had had a visit from Mrs. Kelsie and they had enjoyed discussing various books they had both read and recommending new titles to each other. Some on his list were, in fact, books she had suggested.

"She's an extremely interesting woman, don't you think, James?" Henry inquired, his eyes bright and laughing behind his thick lenses.

I smiled back and said nothing.

Henry's eyes seemed to dominate his physical presence. It was from this part of him that his inner light radiated outwards to the world. These intense blue eyes were indeed the mirror of his soul. These eyes showed no evidence of any fear. This was a man, who I felt sure, had found a complete knowingness and trust. He had come through his personal traumas and found enlightenment. He was totally at ease with himself and his environment. He had peace of mind and an acceptance that he was just where he was meant to be in each moment.

The wonder of it all was that while I was near this warm quiet man, I too felt at peace and shared in this certainty and feeling of complete surrender and trust that surrounded and filled his being.

I hoped that perhaps someday, I would be fortunate enough to have this feeling, filling my being in every moment.

Henry's voice interrupted my thoughts, "Are you ready to face next door? He'll be waiting for you—though he won't tell you that. I just want you to know that what you have done has already made a difference. It's not visible to the naked eye but, if Harry was under a microscope, you would be able to see that a change for the better had begun. I wanted you to know this, so don't be put off by a seeming lack of progress."

This was the encouragement I needed to hear and, with my spirits lifted I returned to the car to collect the red plastic tray, which contained the untidy selection of books, for a man who said he had no interest in them. Nestling inside one book was a tiny gold star—a glimmer of light—a hidden treasure—secretly smuggled into the darkness of number eight Oak Walk.

Harry received me much as before but I sensed, under his aggressive manner, a reign of caution. There was within Harry, a fear that if he pushed me too far, I might turn on my heel and disappear with the red tray and its contents, under my arm. Because of this, he did not wish to detain me and I was on my way, empty handed, in a matter of minutes, promising to return for the books in three weeks time.

I felt a bit frustrated at how slowly everything was going and how out of my control it all was.

In order to cheer myself up, I decided to ring Mrs. Kelsie—Frances—and ask her out as soon as I returned to the office. I was surprised at how disappointed I felt when there was no answer at her number.

FOURTEEN

Two days later, when I was showing out a new client, I was startled to find a flushed Mrs. Palmer hovering in the front office—shopping trolley in tow. Fiona inquired, as the door closed behind our client, if I could possibly spare Mrs. Palmer a few minutes. She had waited in the hope that I could see her between appointments.

I held the door wide and ushered her into my office, the faithful shopper at her heels! I had often thought that there must be an art to controlling one of these contraptions in order to achieve such dexterity and manoeuvrability.

As soon as the door had closed, my co-conspirator gave me an up to the minute verbal report. The crux of it was, that that morning, when she had been 'doing' for Mr. Boswell, she had at once observed that the books had been disturbed. They were in piles instead of in a row on their sides. Mr. Boswell, had apparently looked at them all and more than that, one book, a gardening one, was on the floor beside his chair. Mrs. Palmer, bursting with excitement, went on, "Would you believe it, Mr. Fanshaw? I was just so excited, I can tell you—I just had to come straight round and tell you. Thank goodness you were here! Now I must fly or I'll be late back with the shopping. I'll keep you posted." And without giving me time to say anything, she was off with a flurry of air and with a neat twist of her wrist—she and her companion on wheels were gone.

What a woman! No one looking at her would dream she had so many thousands of pounds carefully invested on my instruction. She could have done her shopping in a chauffeur driven limousine, if she'd had a mind to.

When I had heard winners of large sums of money being

interviewed, saying that they would not let it change their lives, I had smiled cynically, and laughed at their naivety—but here was the wonderful Mrs. Palmer doing just that!

I had to admit to feelings of excitement at the turn of events at number eight Oak Walk. I had not dared to hope for such progress so soon. I doubted that Harry would admit to any interest in the books and when I spoke to the home-help later that week, I realised that this was indeed so.

She saw me in the street and she burst out, without preamble, as was her way, "The cunning old sod—when I got back with the shopping, he had put all the books back as you'd left them—more or less. I must have caught him off guard that morning. Still we know what we know…."

She put her forefinger up and tapped the side of her nose and winked at me and off she went again.

I was able to recount all of this to Frances, the following week. I'd eventually got hold of her and we had met for a drink one evening, in a local wine bar. She had been away for a few days visiting friends in the Lake District. She was keeping well and the doctors were delighted with her progress. She had been advised to avoid any lifting for six months, so she would not be returning to her library duties until after that. I had to admit that I was glad to hear this. I was not ready to hand back Oak Walk as yet. I felt this venture had still much to teach me.

I had mentioned to Frances, at our last meeting, that as my library card supplied the books for Harry every month, I had no borrowing power left for myself. I shouldn't have been surprised, therefore, when she arrived at the wine bar with two books, under her arm, for me to borrow. She said, "I have shelves of books at home. I hope you will feel free to read whichever you want while Harry makes up his mind to borrow books on his own account. We'll have to celebrate when that day comes!"

It was towards the end of the following week that I had more news from the inside of number eight. I was sitting quietly on the bench under the oak tree enjoying some late autumn sunshine. The tree had lost most of its leaves by this time and they were scattered all over the grass—a wonderful carpet of colour. The child in me loved to hear the crackling sound they made under my feet. I was lost in thought—far away—nowhere in particular—enjoying being, rather than doing—when I heard the familiar sound of the wheels of a shopping trolley, and a contrived cough from Mrs. Palmer.

"Nothing to report," she said in a low voice, "but I know he's reading the books. I can tell. There's a difference in him. He's got a secretive look about him. I found something strange to day on his bedroom carpet."

She opened her hand and there in her palm glinted the tiny golden star. I smiled but said nothing.

"I'm going to keep it for luck," she said. "It's a good omen, don't you think?"

"Indeed I do." I agreed as I lifted my hand in a friendly farewell.

This was news indeed. I now knew that Harry had opened a book in his bedroom. He must be reading that dark covered book—what was it called?—'A million lights in the darkness'—something like that! And I knew for sure that the small light, lost within Harry, had turned up to another level.

As I made my way to Harry's door on the following Wednesday, I had to keep a check on my rising excitement. I must not expect too much.

On the surface, everything at number eight seemed much as before. Harry was just as unsociable and ungracious as ever. He still sat hunched in his chair with his back turned to me, but I knew his attention was fully focused on my presence in his room. The one thing I did notice was that he turned down the volume on the television as I entered—this was progress!

I read down the list of titles, as I had last time, and Harry, with a seeming disinterest, rattled off scores for each title in turn. Again, I was aware that there was more thought behind his responses than his outward manner showed. I did learn that he had no interest in the western, Winston Churchill or the murder mystery—he gave them a score of one. The gardening books and the one about tropical fish scored threes and the rest were twos. Harry also gave a score of one, to the little black book covered in stars, but I knew he had read it and I also knew what he felt about it. I did not require a lie detector to tell me that he felt emotional when he thought about this book.

Harry couldn't wait to see the back of me, and had no difficulty in getting rid of me. He did not dare to be as rude as he normally was as he had an underlying fear that I might not return. His parting words, "I suppose you'll be back next week," in a long suffering tone, held a pathetic hidden plea of, 'you won't forget will you?'

"I'll be back." I said, "thank you for helping me again." There was a lump in my throat, as I closed the door on this sad, desperately lonely, old man.

When I got back to the library and gathered the books together, I realised that there were only nine books in the tray. I must have dropped one. I searched the back of the car, but it was empty. I scanned the books and tried to ascertain which book was missing. I looked down the list and, when I realised that it was the book covered in stars which was missing, I knew, without a shadow of doubt, where it was. Harry had been unable to let it go. He had somehow managed to remove it from the tray. No wonder he had hurried me out. He was afraid I would notice that the tray was one book short.

I felt so glad that he had kept the book. It didn't matter. I would just arrange a renewal on it and choose nine books instead of ten for next week's delivery. There would be no need to mention this to Harry. I would wait and see how he wanted to deal with it.

FIFTEEN

Frances had gone away again and I was surprised at how much I missed her. It wasn't that we had seen much of each other, it was more that I missed knowing she was there, if I wanted to talk to her.

She sent me a post card. I don't know how she had managed to find it. The picture was of a magnificent oak tree, covered in wonderful green foliage and the sun was shining through a single leafy section making it brighter than all the rest. I couldn't believe it. I imagined Frances' delight when she found it. She said she would be back home the following Tuesday and would I like to have dinner with her, later that week. She promised to ring me and arrange it, when she got back. The child in me wanted to whoop and skip again and I found myself smiling at odd times throughout the day.

There was a difference in the office these days, and it wasn't only because of the orange curtains and the house plants. Without realising it I had, as Henry had suggested 'lightened up'. I was much less formal and business-like and I could tell that Julia and Fiona were less intimidated by me. We all smiled more and the atmosphere in the office was more relaxed. It had happened gradually. I had mellowed and softened and was more easy-going and, to my surprise, standards had not dropped, business had not taken a down turn, in fact it had never been better. It seemed strange that I was giving my work less of my attention and yet achieving better results!

I was leaving the office the following Tuesday and was just about to switch off the lights when my attention was drawn to one of the plants. It was a small bonsai in a shallow green pot. I had bought it a few weeks ago, fascinated by its tree like features in miniature form. It did not look well, some of the leaves looked yellow and ready to drop off. The soil was moist. I stared at it. "What's the matter with you?" I said aloud, startling myself. As I spoke, I looked around to reassure myself that there was nobody there to hear me. I didn't know what to do and decided that the only thing I could do was to move the little tree and give it a different position in the room. Perhaps it was in a draught. I lifted it carefully and began searching for a new location.

"Where would you prefer?" I asked, "perhaps some company?" I moved into the outer office and set the sad little tree on the window ledge beside a happy looking spider plant.

I returned home and throughout the evening I was surprised at how my mind kept returning to the picture of that bonsai plant. What was this all about? I asked myself. It was surely more than the revelation that I now spoke to plants—nothing particularly remarkable in that. Everyone knew that even The Prince of Wales did that!

When I awoke next morning I knew what I was going to do. I would ask Harry to look after the bonsai tree for me. He looked after my books, now he could help me with my unhappy plant.

That day, being the fourth Wednesday in the month, I was on my way back to Oak Walk—my car laden with trays of books. This time, beside me, on the front passenger seat, inside a little cardboard box, sat my sad little bonsai tree—a bit like a beloved pet on the way to the vets, I thought.

This brought back a long forgotten memory of myself, as a little boy, clutching a small cardboard box with holes in it, containing an injured blackbird. I had found it in the garden. I had insisted, much to my father's annoyance, that we take it to the vets. The bird died as the vet examined it. He said it was from shock. I nearly cried, but held back the tears. The vet was kind and said I had done the right thing. I still remember my father saying, he'd known the bird would die and going to the vets was a stupid waste of time. I really felt I hated my father that day.

It was strange how I kept dredging up these long suppressed emotions and having a closer look at them. I guessed this was what happened during psychotherapy. I was beginning to have a vague understanding of how healing a process this might be. It was as if I could now validate feelings which up until now had been suppressed and invalidated.

My regular calls completed without incident, I made my way towards Harry's door, the cardboard box, containing the bonsai, perched on top of the books. Harry's curtains were opened only a few inches as usual. He called for me to come in and I made my way into the front room.

The first thing I noticed was the missing book waiting on the edge of the sideboard. "You must have dropped that one when you left last week." Harry said, before I had time to comment.

"Oh I thought I must have done. I realised when I got back to the library that I was one book short. I've renewed it, so will just leave it here with these new ones." I responded.

Harry's eyes were on the cardboard box, balanced on top of the books.

"What have you got there? Not more junk to clutter up my place?" he grumbled.

"Well, actually," I said, "I am going to ask another favour of you. You've been so good helping me out with the books, I wondered if you could help me out with this plant of mine. I bought it for the office—to cheer the place up a bit and it's not looking too happy." I moved towards Harry opening the box and holding it out to him saying, "I don't know what I'm doing wrong—maybe its the artificial light or too much or too little water. I don't know. I'm no authority on plants. I just wondered if you could keep an eye on it for a week or two. See if you could save it. It's a bonsai tree." I held my breath.

"Let's get it out of the box so as I can see what all the fuss is about! I haven't got all day, you know." With gentle hands, he carefully lifted the bonsai out of the box and looked at the plant closely, and said, "Oh dear, what have you been doing to this? This is a very sick looking tree." His old hands touched the soil and his twisted fingers brushed the leaves. With great tenderness he felt the leaves and tiny branches. These were a gardener's fingers. This was a man in tune with things that grew. I imagined I could feel the plant respond to this, just as a sick animal responds to the knowing touch of a vet.

"You'd best leave it here, then" Harry went on. "I can't say if it can be saved but I can't do any worse than you've done. Can I?" I felt as if I was being categorised along with child abusers and animal torturers, at the very least.

"Thanks, so much, Mr. Boswell." I grovelled. "I didn't know who else to ask. Would it be all right if I called in next week to see how it's doing?" Again, I held my breath.

"I suppose so. If you must. But make sure it's in the afternoon. I'll see you then." Harry had had enough.

I was on my way—the books for now had taken a back seat and the pathetic little bonsai was the energy worker at number eight for the time being. I had great hopes for this little tree.

I knew that I had been well guided and, each time this happened, I became a little more trusting in my ability to pick up on the directions and signs, as they were presented to me.

Not only was I becoming a more feeling and emotional being, I was also growing into a more intuitive person. I was beginning to quite like this new improved James Fanshaw. I realised then, that until now, I had never really liked myself very much.

SIXTEEN

The following evening I was due to have dinner with Frances. I arrived on time, carrying a bottle of wine, and her books. She was looking very well and I could tell that her holiday had done her good. While she was finishing off preparations in the kitchen, I became immersed in the contents of her bookshelves. I was so engrossed in this that I did not hear her call me and almost jumped out of my skin when she tapped me on my shoulder. The book I had lifted down and was lost in was all about auras, energies, colours and light. I felt like a petulant schoolchild being dragged away from a favourite television programme, by a strict parent.

I said this to Frances and we both laughed.

Never in my life had I found conversation so easy or so satisfying. We were so in tune with thoughts and ideas. It felt as if I had tapped into a whole new dimension and there would never be enough time for me to explore, absorb and experience it all.

Frances had made this discovery not too long ago and knew exactly how it was making me feel. She was reliving it all again in me. There are few things so exciting and exhilarating as sharing in such moments of enlightenment and understanding, with another person. It must be like great moments in science when a desired result occurs after months and months of research and experiment that moment when you call out 'Eureka!' When two or more minds are able to share in such an experience the power, satisfaction and joy must be increased.

The meal was good, and the wine a perfect choice, but we both knew that had we been eating bread and cheese served with orange squash, it would not have made any difference to the evening.

We shared thoughts, beliefs and ideas on another level—not

mental, not intellectual, perhaps spiritual—that does not describe it either, and to say we had a philosophical discussion does not describe it at all.

I left later that evening—clutching an armful of books and feeling truly contented and at peace with life in that moment.

Just as the changes in me seemed to accelerate after a slow and faltering start, so did the changes in Harry Boswell.

Each time we met, following the introduction of the bonsai tree to Harry's care, I was aware of some change for the better, however small, in his attitude or in his surroundings.

We were now into November and the days were cold. I still walked most days and these walks always included Oak Walk. I occasionally stopped and sat by the oak tree but, in these cooler, damper days it was less frequent and I saw little of Henry apart from my library delivery days.

However, as it happened, two days after I had left my bonsai with Harry, I was sitting on the bench under the oak tree and was enjoying an unexpected burst of winter sunshine. I had closed my eyes in order to fully enjoy the sensation of heat on my face. I was trying to imagine Harry and my bonsai tree. I was counting the days until I could call at number eight again. It was as if a close friend was in an isolation ward and was not allowed visitors for a week.

I started, as a voice I knew well said, "You are deep in thought!" I opened my eyes, delighted to see Henry lowering himself carefully into the space beside me. "Have you noticed the curtains?" he said, his eyes directing me to Harry's window.

A surge of delight went through me and I said, "He's opened them wide! I can't believe it!" We both sat there—sharing the moment—both with expressions of smug satisfaction on our faces.

"How did you do it?" Henry inquired.

"He's opened them for the bonsai." I said, knowing that this was exactly why Harry had pulled back his curtains and let the sunshine into his home for the first time. I went on to explain to Henry about my unhappy and sickly plant and how I had put it into Harry's expert hands.

Henry was beaming, "Perfect" he said, "just perfect!" and he was on his feet and heading home.

I sat on, smiling—deep within, a warm glowing feeling seemed to fill my being. I wanted to keep this moment with me for ever. The sun went behind a dark cloud, but its brightness and warmth remained with me. No cloud could darken this moment!

When I called on Harry the following Wednesday, I was expecting to see a thriving, happy bonsai tree. The improvement I saw was certainly not in the sickly plant. It, to my eyes, looked worse than ever. Harry, on the other hand, was thriving. The first thing I noticed was that the television was switched off and the source of light was the window. The sad little plant sat on the window sill—it was smaller and barer than before.

Harry saw my disappointment, and in an exasperated voice, said, "Give me a chance. I told you it was in a bad way. I've had to cut it back and it needs to recover from that. It needs time now and encouragement and cheering up!"

Coming from Harry, who could have depressed for Britain up until now, this was ironic.

"It needs to be in the light. I put it in this window in the morning then move it to the bedroom to get the late afternoon sun if there is any. We should begin to see an improvement in a week or so. Just wait and see." Harry encouraged.

This man must have been given a personality transplant! He had not only been civil, but had just come out with a positive statement. I couldn't believe it!

"That's great." I said. I was at a complete loss for words. "Thank you so much, Mr. Boswell. I'll see you both next week."

I had to get out, I could feel another whoop and skip coming on. I was bursting with excitement.

When something wonderful happens, there is a great need to share it. There was only one person who would understand what this meant to me and the full meaning of what had occurred. I would ring her right away, from the office. She just had to be in.

When her newly acquired answering machine responded, I felt

so let down—almost angry with Frances. Where was she? Why wasn't she there? Again I was plunged back to a childhood memory—I was a small boy, rushing home from school with some important news. I could not recall what it was—but I had this bursting need to share it with my mother and she wasn't there. A neighbour had been asked to look out for me and keep an eye on me until my mother returned. The shine had gone from the moment and I couldn't get it back. I sulked and was angry with my mother and she had no idea why and I could not have explained it to her even if I had wanted to.

The difference now was that I would not sulk with Frances and I would be able to explain how I'd felt and, best of all, I knew she would understand.

We were into December and the weather was cold and the days short. I had one more library delivery before Christmas. They were to keep the books for an extra week to cover the holiday period and could have extra books if they wished.

Harry, of course, would have his regular tray and an extra visit. I hoped he would not notice that he was having different treatment. Now that his curtains were open he would be more likely to see what I was up to.

The day before I was due at Oak Walk, I was walking my usual route—it was a particularly cold, damp morning and I was walking briskly to keep warm—no sitting on benches under oak trees to-day. As I passed the row of houses on Oak Walk, my attention was caught by a knocking from Harry's front window. To my amazement, he was gesturing furiously and beckoning me to come inside. I wondered what sort of emergency had occurred, as I hurried through his door.

"I was watching out for you." Harry said, "I didn't know if you'd be coming by—it being so cold and wet. I wanted you to see this." He gestured to the window ledge and the bonsai tree. "What do you think?" he said, as he watched me.

I went over to take a closer look and immediately saw what all the excitement was about. A tiny new leaf had sprouted—the first sign of new life since its drastic pruning. I turned and beamed at Harry saying, "Well done. I have to admit I thought you had killed it. You're a genius—a miracle worker!"

Harry was feeling good and said, "The wife always told me that when I got plants to recover. When she went...." His voice saddened, "I just seemed to give up. I let my garden go. I deserted all my beautiful roses. There didn't seem any point any more. I never thought I would feel this thrill again. I thought perhaps I'd lost my touch. It's been touch and go, I can tell you. It's needed intensive care all right but it'll be fine from now on." These were the most revealing words I had heard Harry say since I'd met him.

"I'm so glad you caught me." I replied. "This has made my day." I gestured to the recovering plant—but it was more than that little green leaf that had made me glow inside. "I'll see you both tomorrow. Keep up the good work." I said as I made for the door. I was on my way back to the office and it was as if the sun was shining!

SEVENTEEN

In the run up to Christmas—a season I usually tried to ignore—the girls put up decorations in the office for the first time. We even had a small tree in the corner of the front office. This, I suppose, was a follow on from the orange curtains and the house plants.

One morning I noticed that Fiona was looking less than her usual cheerful self and asked if there was anything wrong.

"Yes," she said, "I'm proper fed up, if you must know. Me and my Bert have been asked away for Christmas. It's a real posh affair—in a big hotel. Three nights that's all—and he says we can't go, because of Princess! We've got no one to mind her and he won't put her into kennels. My folks haven't the time to look after her with all the family descending for the holiday. And Bert's family don't like dogs—not even well behaved ones like our Princess. It's hopeless! I don't suppose you'd fancy having a friendly greyhound around for Christmas would you, Mr. Fanshaw?" she said, smiling at her own cheek. She hadn't meant to say this. I knew that feeling when words come out of your mouth, bypassing the brain. It happened to me more and more these days. And, to my horror, it happened again and I seemed to be saying I would get involved!

"I don't know anything about dogs, I'm afraid, but I do know someone who might help me to look after Princess!"

"Are you serious?" Fiona said, her face lighting up. It dimmed again almost immediately, as she said, "Bert won't leave her with just anyone. He dotes on that dog. I do too, but with him it's more of an obsession.

Does this friend of yours know about dogs?"

"Well, yes," I replied, "he used to own one. I believe he is a relative of yours. He lives in Oak Walk—Mr. Harry Boswell!"

Fiona's face crumpled. It was as if I had played a most cruel joke on her—raised her hopes, then dashed them completely.

"You mean Bert's grandfather?" she said crossly. "That old misery. He'd never do ought for anyone! Anyway he's too old—he couldn't take himself out, let alone a dog. And another thing, they won't be allowed animals, not in sheltered housing…. That's why he had to get rid of his dog. Cruel, that is, making old folks leave their pets. I always said that shouldn't be allowed! We took his old dog in, but she pined and didn't last long. It was ever so sad."

"Well, he owes you a favour then," I said. "Let me have a word with him. I've got to know him recently and if I agreed to do the dog walking, and he knows how to look after a dog, we could surely manage the three days between us. I've nothing much planned over Christmas."—Nothing at all, if the truth were known. But if this wild plan took off, I was going to be fully occupied.

I felt that my mouth had run away with me this time. I couldn't believe what I had suggested. This was a million miles from library books or even a bonsai tree. Well, I would just have to put it to Harry now. Fiona was already on the telephone to 'her Bert' and if he gave the go ahead, I would be forced to tell Harry what I'd done. I was hoping against hope that Bert would not entertain such a proposal for the temporary care of his precious greyhound.

As soon as Fiona came into my office, smiling from ear to ear, I knew that she had persuaded Bert to agree.

"Bert says, if you can persuade his grandfather to have Princess, he will agree to you doing the dog walking, and we can have our fancy Christmas! Oh, Mr. Fanshaw, do you think there's a chance that he'll say yes?" She was imagining it all already.

I very much doubted that Harry would entertain any of this, but I didn't say so. All I did say was that I would speak to Mr. Boswell the following day and let her know the outcome.

I was extremely aware of the risk I would be running in pushing Harry too far or too quickly. I could, so easily, lose the delicate balance our relationship had reached. I was uncertain, as to how to approach this business of Christmas and Princess. I felt he might see this as some kind of conspiracy between myself and his family and a gross interference. I doubted that he would believe that this was more coincidence than anything else.

I had gone over various approaches in my head and decided on none. I would just wait and see what happened and trust that the right words would come out of my mouth and that Harry would interpret them in the best way for him. It would either work out, or it wouldn't. This was what I told myself, but I was none the less in quite an agitated state when I knocked on Harry's door the next day.

He wasn't surprised to see me as I was armed with the usual tray of books. We dealt with these quickly and I went to admire the bonsai. It did look better every time I saw it. I was obviously ill at ease and Harry said, "Is there anything wrong?"

"Yes," I said, "I think I have done something very stupid and you'll probably go mad at me. Will you just hear me out—don't say anything until I've finished. Then you can yell at me!"

I had obviously got his full attention and he nodded, agreeing to my terms. My mouth worked overtime—a bit like Mrs. Palmers'. The facts came out just as it had all happened. The fact that I had discovered that one of my secretaries was married to his grandson, Bert Boswell, and that they needed to find someone to mind their dog over Christmas, and how Fiona, jokingly, and as a last resort, had asked me. And what I had said without thinking and how I had mentioned that he might help me, as I knew nothing about dogs etc. etc.... The whole story poured out like water from a tap. I finished with an apology for mentioning his name in all this which was, with hindsight, a crazy scheme. I said, "I'll tell Fiona it just isn't possible—but I promised I would mention it to you. I am really sorry. I don't know what I was thinking about—put it down to pre-Christmas madness!"

I stopped. I had not dared to look at Harry's face, while I spoke. I lifted my eyes now, ready for the onslaught!

He was deep in thought and didn't look angry. He just looked incredibly sad. I had opened old wounds—family—Christmases—his dog. What had I done? This was unforgivable!

Our eyes met and he saw my pain and knew I shared his. We were mirrors for each other. He sighed deeply and said quietly,

"Well this wants some thinking about. You know the Council don't allow us to have pets here, don't you? I've no time for all that red tape, bureaucracy nonsense. I've broken the odd bye-law in my time and we're only talking about a few days—didn't you say?"

I nodded, I couldn't believe it. He was actually considering my proposal!

"Now let's see," he went on. "I couldn't exercise the dog—you would have to do that—twice a day. I could let her out the back door between walks, if needs be. I'd manage the feeding and she could sleep on the floor in my room at night. Nobody need know. Yes, it could work. You are sure our Bert thought I was up to it? I know how he dotes on that dog. Well, well, this is a turn up for the books—you me and Princess spending the Christmas holiday together! Who'd have thought it? I certainly didn't know what I was letting myself in for when I let you and your bloody books through my door. I bet you didn't either!" and he laughed. It stopped in his throat, it had been unused for so long and it took him by surprise. He turned it into a cough. "You'd better go now. I need to think about all of this. Ask Bert to call round after work to discuss it all. Tell him to bring Princess with him so that we can see if we like each other. Dogs like me as a rule—more than people, some would say!"

I left Oak Walk in a daze. I returned the books from the other residents to the library and chatted to Mr. MacKenzie in a sort of trance. I felt I was functioning on auto pilot.

As I entered the office, two pairs of eyes were fixed on me. Fiona and Julia were awaiting my return with unprecedented interest.

"Well....?" Fiona couldn't contain herself. My expression was giving nothing away.

"Yes—he said yes!" I said smiling. "I can't get over it! He wants Bert to go round tonight, with the dog, to finalise arrangements!"

"Oh, thank you, thank you, Mr. Fanshaw. You are an angel!" and to both our surprise, and the amazement of Julia, Fiona threw her arms round my neck and kissed me!

I hurriedly escaped into my office and tried to turn my attention to matters of business. It was not easy as my emotions were all over the place. However the world of finance and columns of figures have a power all of their own. They demand and expect full concentration and attention. They were the ideal antidote to my recent exploits and raised emotions.

It seemed no time at all until Fiona popped her head around my door and announced that she and Julia were going home and that she had spoken to 'her Bert' and he would be going round to Oak Walk that evening to see his grandfather. It really looked as if they could have their dream Christmas after all.

I finished my work in progress and then found myself lost in thought. My Christmas looked like being busier than usual this year. I had to admit I was glad. I was one of those thousands of single people who found Bank Holidays and such times, very difficult. These were times which made you feel very alone, isolated and unloved, even though you were quite content with single status, for the rest of the year. At such times you somehow didn't fit in and were rather odd and a bit pathetic.

I had, in the past, tried going away for Christmas and New Year and had found this even more depressing. Now I opted to stay quietly at home—catching up on work, jobs around the house, watching television and now, I had my reading. However, this Christmas I would have visits to Harry and dog walking to help fill the days.

Frances was spending Christmas and New Year with friends in Wales. We went out to dinner two nights before she left and I was able to tell her all about Bert and Fiona, Harry and Princess. She said she would spare me a thought as she sat sipping mulled wine by a large log fire! Before we left the restaurant, we arranged to meet after she returned, so that she could hear all the details about my unorthodox festivities!

EIGHTEEN

I could not recall a Christmas quite like this one. In recent years I had adopted the policy that if I ignored it, as much as possible, it would come and go without inconvenience. I went through the motions of sending out annual cards on my list and buying token gifts for the girls in the office and the cleaner. I always received a few gifts, mainly bottles of wine, port and whisky from grateful clients.

However, because of the changes that had taken place within me, I was more emotionally involved somehow. I now mixed with people on a more personal level and, as a result, I felt touched and appreciative when small thoughtful gifts and cards were handed to me.

Fiona and Julia were eager to give me their gifts of my Mr. Happy mug and a little bonsai tree, to replace the one they thought had died. This new one was growing in a shallow blue Chinese style pot and had a little Buddha-like figure perched beneath the tiny, yet perfect tree. I was delighted with both gifts and was able to express this long forgotten emotion.

Mrs. Palmer burst into the front office, the week before Christmas, with the inevitable shopping trolley at her heels. She produced, from the depths of the shopper, a cake tin which she held out to me accompanied by a huge smile, "I've made you a Christmas cake, just to say thank you for all your help. I hope you like fruit cake!"

I was so touched by this gesture, a part of me wanted to hug Mrs. Palmer but I managed to contain myself. There was still too much of the old, retiring, unemotional me left. My delighted facial expression and the sincerity in my voice, as I thanked her, was all that was needed.

The unexpected gifts did not stop there. Although I had met my clients at Oak Walk, only a few times, they seemed to have drawn me in to their circle of friends. Perhaps they just wanted to show their appreciation to me like you do to the milkman, the dustbinmen and the paperboy. It felt more than this. The thoughtfulness of their cards and gifts, told me that.

Mr. Paterson, had searched through his favourite books—ones he had clung on to even though he knew he would never be able to read their print again and he had chosen one specially for me. He had written a charming message inside the cover. This meant so much to me and I knew I would treasure this book and think of him every time I saw it on my book shelf. I told him this and he seemed pleased.

Miss Bryson, perhaps, surprised me most of all. With her severe and schoolmarmish manner, it was not easy to tell if you had met with her approval and reached her high standards of behaviour. However, the beautifully hand-stitched and mounted card, which she gave me, let me know she thought I was reasonably competent and worthy of encouragement. She was pleased with my response and touched when later, I told her that I had put her card in a frame and kept it on my desk.

Mr. and Mrs. Sinclair had a gift, wrapped in Christmas paper, waiting for me. "Just a little something to open on Christmas morning," he said, "You've been so kind to us and all the others." Mrs. Sinclair nodded and gave me one of her lovely, lop-sided smiles.

I was beginning to realise one of the real joys of voluntary work—not the presents but the heartfelt appreciation from those you help. I realised that when someone is paid to help, it is never the same. It is just their job. These gifts were not meant as payment for bringing the library books—these were a mark of appreciation of me, as a person. It made me feel wonderful.

Henry too had a gift for me. It was not wrapped—in fact he lifted it down from his shelf and gave it to me saying, "Someone gave this to me many years ago and I want you to have it now." It was a little oil-filled lamp with a glass shade. "It works beautifully," he said, "and why I was given it and why I am now giving it to you, is that when you adjust that wheel on the side, the light gets brighter and brighter." He smiled and looked deeply into my eyes. My eyes, full of tears and pleasure, smiled back into his.

Years later, when I turn up my little lamp, I am back in that moment in Henry's radiant front room and I can see those eyes still smiling into mine.

I closed the office officially on the evening before Christmas Eve and that year we had wine and some of Mrs. Palmer's Christmas cake, as a pre-Christmas celebration. The three of us raised our glasses to each other and exchanged gifts.

The cake was wonderful. I was inordinately pleased with this gift and realised that this was the first cake I had ever had baked for me. Even as a small boy, I had always had bought cake. I don't recall my mother ever baking a cake. I used to feel so envious when, at other children's parties, they had birthday cakes lovingly made for them by their mothers. They probably envied me my beautiful bought cakes, iced and decorated by professional hands.

Fiona was very excited about her holiday with Bert. She told me that they would drop Princess off at Oak Walk the next morning. She would already have had her morning walk and if I could go round about tea time and take her out then she would be fine until the following morning. I told her this would be no problem.

I was feeling quite excited about this dog walking assignment and could not wait to meet the delightful Princess. I hoped she would take to me and would not mind taking her walks with a total stranger.

This feeling of excited anticipation was once again, almost a childlike emotion. I was excited and yet apprehensive. I was also very relieved that Harry—a man who knew about dogs, was in charge, for the most part, of Princess's welfare.

NINETEEN

When I knocked on the plain green door of number eight Oak Walk, just after five p.m. on Christmas Eve, I was greeted by Harry's voice—stronger than usual but also lighter, more gentle in tone, telling me to come in and close the door. There was the accompanying bark of a fairly large dog. It was fortunate, I thought, that Harry Boswell had only one adjoining neighbour and that that neighbour was Henry. A less agreeable neighbour might have been quick to report the unlawful presence of a pet next door.

Harry was in his usual seat. His left hand rested gently on the dog's collar and in a low tender voice, he spoke to the dog, "It's all right, Princess. This is a friend. Say hello to Mr. Fanshaw."

The dog relaxed and welcomed me with a friendly look from her large trusting brown eyes. She was a beautiful animal—sleek and angular, with a shiny coat of the softest colour, somewhere between cream and gold. Her head was pointed and thin and her mouth seemed set in a wide smile, as her pink tongue protruded and gave me a welcoming lick. I liked her at once and felt that she had trusted Harry's description of me as a friend and had settled for that.

"She's lovely." I said. "She looks at home here already!"

"She's a real beauty and no mistake." Harry said proudly. "A credit to our Bert, I must say. He was always good with animals, even as a small boy—not like his Dad in that respect. He didn't seem to get along with creatures at all, something lacking in him. Never trust anyone who doesn't like animals, I always say. I can see you have a liking for dogs. She's taken to you right away!"

I felt unduly pleased at this and said, " I've not had much to do with dogs, I must confess. I always used to dream of having a dog of my own, when I was a boy—but was never allowed one. I wasn't allowed any pets." As I said this I felt the sadness I had felt as a young boy, denied his dream. I had been an only child. I felt his loneliness and his longing and need for someone or something to share his life and ease his feelings of isolation. As I stroked the soft coat and looked into the dog's eyes, I knew that having such a companion would have filled a huge emptiness in that little boy's early existence.

Harry Boswell had blossomed with the arrival of his house guest. He seemed to have lost ten years or more. He moved more easily—held himself straighter and had acquired a purposefulness and direction that he had never shown before.

"Pass me the lead, would you?" he said. "It's on the table. I'll put it on. You'd best keep her on the lead—we don't want to lose her, do we? Bert says she'll be no trouble and she seems well disciplined and obedient, but we won't take any chances. Will you be able to give her about an hour's walk, do you think? I wish I was able to come with you both...." He looked wistfully into the distance, remembering how it used to be....

Princess was eager to be off now that her lead was on. Her beautiful angular body was meant for exercise. Her long limbs moved with an extraordinary gracefulness. She walked dutifully beside me, adapting her steps to my strides. I was glad to walk quickly—it was cold with a slight dampness in the air.

We headed for the park—I had planned the route—round the recreation field, down the tow path to the Navigation Inn—across the bridge at the bottom lock and back up the opposite tow path to the cricket field—then back home past the library.

It was early evening—Christmas Eve. Everyone seemed to be hurrying, rushing home carrying last minute packages—off to stay with family—coming from, or going to parties. There were fairy lights in the trees and lanterns strung alongside the canal. I had never seen the town look so beautiful and I was out walking with a Princess! I found myself smiling to myself as I walked.

As we passed the church, the stained glass windows were lit up from within and I could hear the strains of organ music and Christmas Carols sung in children's voices. The dog looked up at me with those sad brown eyes above her smiling mouth and we shared in the special magic.

Why, I asked myself, had I forgotten my childhood longing for a canine companion? Why, when I became an adult, had I never thought of having a dog of my own? Without realising, I had taken on my parents' attitudes and ideals. I had remained safe inside the boundaries set by them and, until now, I had had no idea what I was missing!

The sadness of missed opportunities and wasted years was quickly replaced by the joy I had found in this moment and many similar moments which I had experienced over the last few months!

We were heading home now and the dog seemed to sense this, even though it was not to the home either of us was used to. We quickened our pace and were soon walking under the oak tree and nearing number eight. I saw Harry standing in his lighted window, watching out for us. I raised my hand in recognition.

Princess greeted Harry and he fussed over her. There was a bond between the two of them and I felt excluded for a moment.

"You'll have a Christmas drink with me?" Harry asked. "Something to warm you on a night like this?" He gestured to an inviting bottle of scotch and two glasses, which he had ready on a table next to his chair.

"Thank you." I said, "that's just what I need." We raised our glasses and drank each others health. Princess lay contentedly between us.

When I had finished my drink, I got up to go, arranging to see them both next morning. I left the two of them totally content by the gas fire. As I walked away, I glanced back at the curtained window. This window had the warmest glow in the entire row. I felt a similar glow inside myself and knew it wasn't just caused by the whisky!

Christmas day was a bright, frosty day—everything sparkled and glinted and how glad I was to have an appointment to keep.

This time at number eight, I was greeted with a welcoming bark from Princess—she was on her feet and eager to be off. Harry looked sad to see us go.

It was a good thing that this arrangement was just for two days—it was going to be a big enough wrench for Harry to let go of Princess, after this short duration!

Walking in the daylight, in the winter sunshine, was even more pleasurable. There were few people about—mostly dog walkers, like myself. We all wished one another a Merry Christmas as we passed. I felt as though I belonged to a wonderful, exclusive club of dog owners. I pretended to myself that this beautiful animal was mine.

How I enjoyed that Christmas Day. Twice in the day, I was out and about walking with Princess.

I basked in the cosy quietness of my home. I enjoyed my dinner for one with a sharpened appetite. I stretched out in front of the television, sipping a glass of single malt, and listened to the Queen's Christmas message to the nation. I dozed contentedly by the fire until it was time to wrap up once more and put on my walking shoes.

I could tell that Harry's day had been special too. He and Princess had enjoyed a Christmas dinner, left by Fiona, and had probably spent the afternoon much as I had.

When I returned from our evening walk, Harry and I sat companionably with the emptying bottle of golden nectar between us. Princess stretched out on the carpet at our feet. I pictured Henry, next door, smiling benevolently on us from the other side of the wall.

We ate mince pies and shortbread—home baked I was sure, by the wonderful Mrs. Palmer. I was certain that when she lovingly baked them for Harry, she never imagined that he would be sharing them with her accountant and a large, very beautiful, greyhound.

It was getting late and I was about to get up and make my way home, when Harry put into words what we were both thinking and feeling, "I'm really going to miss her when she goes home tomorrow. I'd forgotten what great company a dog can be."

There was a desolation, a profound sadness, in his voice as he spoke and I again wondered if I had dealt him a cruel blow by allowing him to re-experience this feeling of warmth and companionship which he had forgotten. Harry answered my silent, rhetorical question by saying, "I wouldn't have missed these last few days for anything. I can't tell you what it has meant to me—you'll never know! I feel as if I have emerged from a very dark place indeed, where I have been imprisoned for a long long time. I won't let myself go back there. Your books were the start, you know—the first glimmer of light. I lied to you—I did look at them—even read some of them!" He smiled like a naughty child who'd just confessed to some misdemeanour .

"I knew you had." I said and grinned.

"I knew you knew," he said and we laughed and Princess raised her head and looked at us both and grinned too.

I left soon after. Princess walked me to the door rubbing her head into my side. I wished she was coming home with me.

That evening I sat in the comfort of my room. I had lit the fire and was enjoying its company and its flickering light and crackling sounds. I gazed into the bright coal and reflected over these last few days. I felt peaceful and truly content.

When the fire grew low and only a few glowing embers remained, I reached out for the little lamp Henry had given me. I had filled it with oil and I lit it carefully. As I adjusted the wick, the light became brighter and brighter and the room was filled with a warm golden glow. My eyes closed, perhaps with the heat of the fire—the soothing warmth of the malt whisky and the result of the fresh air and exercise I'd enjoyed earlier. I was totally relaxed and felt filled and surrounded by the golden light. I was at peace with myself and with the whole world.

Next morning—another very cold icy day, I was up and about preparing for my final walk with Princess. I felt a little anxious about Harry and how he would cope with the departure of his temporary companion.

As the dog and I took our last walk, I had time to think and, as we walked briskly in the icy air, I began to see more clearly. I recognised that the change that had occurred within Harry was not now dependent on the outside props—not books—not the bonsai and not even this beautiful animal for his survival. These had all helped in their own way but the light which had started to brighten in Harry would continue without their support. They had instigated the change—nudged the dimmer switch upwards. That growing light within Harry would remain there and continue to grow in strength. The same thing had, after all, happened within myself under the oak tree last winter.

I nodded and spoke to other dog walkers. I was one of them and I was going to miss this routine. I realised the commitment there must be in owning a dog but I also had had a taste of the companionship and the unconditional love a dog could give.

Why, I asked myself again, when I had always wanted a dog, had I never had one? It must have been because of my childhood conditioning—my parents knew best and, even after they had both died, I was still following their guidelines, their choices. They, in their turn, had taken on the lessons taught by their parents. It was sad but very true....

If I really wanted a dog I could have one. My heart raced with excitement at this thought. I was absolutely free—I could do whatever I wanted. It was as if prison bars were falling open. Nothing had changed since yesterday, other than my perspective of how things were. A quotation from a book I had read came into my head, 'It's only a thought and a thought can be changed!'

I wondered how many other restrictions were influencing my life. This experience, this sudden expanse of freedom, was, at first, rather frightening. It opened so many new avenues of choice and this meant change and change brings fear. The walls of my cosy comfort zone had been pulled down and I felt vulnerable and unprotected and on my own. Suddenly, all the restrictions instilled on me from childhood were being questioned. The ideas and opinions of my parents had always, I now realised, been my points of reference and now I had to decide, on my own choices, my own opinions, my own moral code. Was I at last growing up in my late fifties? It was as if I was becoming the questioning, difficult adolescent, forty years too late. How sad and how very peculiar. I felt restless and ill at ease. My head was full of mental arguments. I had a great need to be with Henry MacFarlane. He was the one person who could clarify this muddled thinking for me.

TWENTY

It was actually the last day of the year before I managed to call in at number seven Oak Walk. Henry, of course, had been expecting me!

"What kept you?" was his opening remark, as he opened the door.

I grinned at him and he said, "I received your psychic message a few days ago and wondered when you would show up!"

If I hadn't had time to get used to this uncanny ability of Henry's, I would have been thoroughly unnerved by this. It still utterly amazed me and I did find it unsettling but I could no longer disbelieve that it was happening.

"You had a busy time over Christmas." Henry said. "Such a brightness next door. It did you no harm either, I can see."

I was the one stuck for words. My thoughts were all muddled and I couldn't remember exactly what I wanted to ask Henry. I hoped that he would help me out—but that was not his way.

We sat down, sipping a seasonal coffee, laced with brandy. Neither of us spoke for quite a while—we were both comfortable with this. It was as if we were communicating with one another on a different level—a meeting of minds—no it wasn't that—more a meeting of souls.

Eventually I heard myself say, "I thought I was coming here to ask you lots of questions and get your advice on issues which have been bothering me but somehow, I don't feel I need to any more. It's as if, somewhere inside of me, they have all been dealt with and sorted out. I can't believe this, as I do not know what the answers are. It is very strange!"

Henry smiled knowingly. I could tell that he had felt this way himself a long time ago. "Believe it!" he said. "The hardest thing is learning to trust that this is so. Gradually it becomes easier and, once you can really know that everything is working out exactly as it should be, in the perfect time, place and sequence, you will find a deep peacefulness enter your life. Listen to the voice inside—learn to go with the ebb and flow of life—surrender, in a way. Above all, enjoy the freedom this gives you as you live in the moment and trust that, whatever comes into your life, you will be able to deal with and learn from.

You have been following your instincts over the last months and just look at what you have achieved! Don't you feel as if you have been part of a giant plan? The choices are always yours. It is just that you will be making them from a deeper or higher part of yourself— no longer the logical, reasoning part of yourself. We follow this path through life—I see it as a movement towards a place of complete fulfillment and enlightenment. This of course can take many lifetimes to achieve!...." He stopped here and I wondered if he felt he had said too much, but I knew he had been guided to drop these words into the pool and allow them to send out ripples and to be there if ever I might have need of them.

As I left Henry's, to my surprise, I was greeted by a bark of welcome from Princess who was just arriving next door. Fiona and Bert, it transpired, were leaving her with Harry overnight. They were having a New Year's Eve party and Harry had offered to share his Hogmanay with Princess. On hearing this, I suggested that I call round next morning and take Princess for her morning walk and allow Bert and Fiona a lie in. Everyone was delighted with this suggestion. My appearance at that exact moment was just another fortunate coincidence—just a touch of synchronicity. Everything in perfect order, in time, place and sequence.

I felt Henry nodding and smiling as he made himself another drink!

As the early weeks of the new year came and went, I entered a period of introspection. My life and work were on an even keel.

I was aware of myself watching myself and my life and trying to be more trustful in the process of life—finding joy in each moment.

I did feel at peace and without struggle. I was not instigating change for change's sake. I did not rush to the nearest animal shelter and pick out a homeless dog. I did not hustle and push Harry. I went on at an even pace neither doing, nor not doing, anything. I was ready to take each moment as it came and to act on my instincts.

My awareness was sharper than ever and, strange as it may seem, my life felt full and fulfilled.

Harry's light continued to grow brighter as the new year progressed. He now selected and discussed his library books and, as a result, was now a bona fide borrower and on the computer, much to Mr. MacKenzie's relief. This meant that I had access to my own ten books should I wish.

Frances and I met up regularly and I was able to share with her many of my innermost thoughts. She allowed me to sound out new ideas and our discussions were long and stimulating. At the same time, I was working my way along her bookshelves.

By the middle of February, Frances was well enough to return to her library duties. I informed Mr. MacKenzie that I did not want a regular delivery position but would be happy to cover for illness or holidays, provided I had sufficient notice.

I had come across some attractive bookmarks and, on the day of my final book deliveries, I gave each person a bookmark as a farewell gift.

TWENTY ONE

It was twelve months since I had first stood beneath the oak tree, at the edge of Oak Walk and how my life had changed in that time. Whatever had occurred, high in the branches above my head, had had a deep and lasting affect on me and on some of the people I had subsequently met.

As the days began to warm and lengthen and I resumed my visits to the bench beneath the tree, I was sometimes joined not only by Henry but, on other occasions, by a much changed Harry.

The door of number eight, usually stood wide open and the curtains were always pulled back. He had a bird feeder by his window and stray cats often visited him and dog walkers would stop and chat. Harry often sat in a deck chair by his door and would speak to everyone. He could manage, on a good day, to walk over to my bench and he and I had many a long chat.

My bonsai tree was the picture of health. I refused to take it back as it seemed to like where it was and because it had done such a wonderful job, I felt it deserved to stay with the man who had saved it.

The dinner ladies delivered the meals-on-wheels with smiles on their faces and a lightness of step and, a certain social worker, called Mercedes, would not have believed it if her successor described the occupant of number eight Oak Walk, as such an agreeable old man!

One evening, towards the end of August, I answered my phone. I was happy to hear Frances' voice on the other end.

I had been feeling out of sorts all day—unable to settle to anything—restless yet sluggish—up one moment, down the next—just out of balance with myself. It was as if I was waiting for something to happen.

When Frances said, "I have some sad news," I knew that this was what I had been sensing. "Henry MacFarlane died this afternoon," she said quietly, "He went quietly and peacefully in his chair. The warden found him."

I felt such a sadness, such a feeling of loss. I had lost someone who had become such an important part of my life. How would I manage without Henry's quiet wisdom, his brightness, his guiding hand?

My grief, I realised, was not for Henry—it had been his time to go to that brightest place of all—the ultimate light he used to speak of with that joyful look in his eyes. My grief was for myself—my loss—the empty void he had left in my world. I had sat on the bench that morning never imagining that my dear friend, Henry, was about to move on and would never sit beside me again.

That evening I sat quietly remembering Henry and what he had meant to me and slowly I began to realise that all he had taught me and all these memories, would never leave me and I knew, with a wonderful certainty, that Henry had not gone far—his wisdom would always be there for me—he had told me, not so long ago, that all my answers were there inside me, waiting to be retrieved at the right time, place and sequence. I felt him saying to me, "All is exactly as it is meant to be in this moment!" He had taught me well.

Henry's funeral was carried out exactly as he had planned it. The disposal of his physical remains was carried out, privately and quickly, with the minimum of fuss. It was obvious that in Henry's opinion, the physical part of him was the least important part of the man who had been here. The worn out shell, of no further use, was buried in the nearby graveyard. He wanted no service or ceremony.

A week after Henry's death, I received an invitation to a gathering at Oak Walk. At first I was horrified at its wording and the irreverence of its tone, then I smiled. This was Henry's doing—his executors were following his wishes to the letter.

The card, which was the brightest yellow—no black bordered invitation—said simply that I was invited to attend Henry MacFarlane's Farewell Party on Tuesday 3rd September at two fifteen p.m. at number Seven Oak Walk. I was pleased that Henry had included my name on his guest list and I was glad that some sort of memorial service—no matter how bizarre was to take place.

The day of Henry's party—no doubt as Henry had arranged—was the most beautiful summer's day with a blue, blue sky and only an occasional white cloud moving across it.

I had arranged to collect Frances, as she too had received a bright yellow invitation. We arrived at Oak Walk just after two. Frances was wearing a brightly patterned sun dress and a flattering straw hat—just right for a garden party.

On the green, in front of Henry's house, were dotted tables and chairs and brightly striped umbrellas. There were trays of glasses and bottles and ice buckets and plates of sandwiches, scones and cakes. I could not help smiling.

"Trust Henry!" Frances whispered.

The guests were all assembled and had taken their seats. I recognised many of the faces there. Mr. Sinclair next to Mrs. Sinclair, in her wheel chair. Mr. Paterson with his newly acquired white stick. Miss Bryson, in neat navy dress with a hand made lace collar, nodded politely in my direction. And Harry Boswell was there, watching everything with considerable interest. He had a pink rose in his buttonhole—he obviously understood what Henry was trying to do.

I recognised other familiar faces—meals-on wheels ladies and a tall, young lady with a ring in her nose and wild colourful hair, who I thought, must be the legendary Mercedes, who had been terrorised by Harry, only a few months ago.

A late comer was hurrying towards the festive group—a smart lady in a cream, well tailored suit. She had a familiar, bustling walk. It was Mrs. Palmer, but there was something different about her. Whatever was it? There was something missing—that was it—she had no shopping trolley at her heels and she looked awkward without it. She breathlessly lowered herself into a vacant chair next to Harry. He shook his head and raised his eyebrows at her in mock exasperation.

I had noticed another face I knew—Mr. Hugh Jenkins. He and his partners had the offices next to mine. He must be Henry's solicitor. He got to his feet. Everyone turned towards him. He had our undivided attention.

"I am Hugh Jenkins—the late Mr. Henry MacFarlane's solicitor and executor of his last will and testament. I welcome you all here, on his behalf," he said in a clear voice. "I have tried to carry out my client's instructions to the letter. I will read out what he wished me to say to you all." He pulled out a single hand written sheet of paper. There wasn't a sound from anyone as he began.

"Dear Friends—thank you for coming here today. I do not wish this to be in any way, a sad or sombre occasion. I have merely invited you here to wish me 'Bon Voyage' and drink a toast to the next part of my journey.

You have all been important to me over the recent years and I valued your help, support and friendship. You all, in different ways, added brightness to my life. So now eat, drink and be merry…." The solicitor paused, then laid aside the piece of paper and said, "Before we do as Henry suggests let me first of all introduce Mr. Matthew MacFarlane—Henry's son."

A tall, sun-tanned man, about my age, got to his feet and spoke in a strong voice with a hint of an Australian accent. "Good afternoon. I don't know if my father will approve of this, but I am going to say a few words anyway. My father was not a religious man but he was an extremely spiritual man. Over the years I have been aware of the changes occurring in him as he grappled and searched for the meaning of his life. In the last years, I believe he had found what he was searching for. I saw in him a certainty and a peace and a profound trust that all was in perfect order. His light was very bright and his warmth and love were a source of great joy to me. It was a great sadness that I lived on the other side of the world, but Dad always used to say, 'we are only a thought apart' and I take great comfort in this, as I firmly believe, that this still holds true." No one moved, but I felt invisible nods of agreement on every side. "He wanted," Henry's son continued, "no sentimentality, no fuss, no funereal dogma and I hope he will forgive me if I finish by reading a verse, by an anonymous writer, that my father always loved." He swallowed and produced a card and began to read,

>"Do not stand by my grave and weep
>I am not there, I do not sleep.
>I am a thousand winds that blow.
>I am the diamond glints on snow.
>I am the sunlight on ripened grain.
>I am the gentle autumn's rain.
>When you awaken in the morning hush,
>I am the swift, uplifting rush of
>Quiet birds in circled flight.
>I am the soft stars that shine at night.
>Do not stand at my grave and cry
>I am not there, I did not die."

There was a moments quiet, then Mr. Jenkins said, "Have you all got a glass? Let's drink to Henry and wish him 'Bon Voyage'." Everyone did so and I knew that everyone there had their own individual special memory of Henry, in their heart, as they raised their glass and said his name.

My eyes were misted and I lifted them upwards to the high branches of the oak tree. It was heavy with leaves which cast a wonderful shadow, protecting us from the hot sun. There was no breeze at all and yet one branch moved and its green leaves danced for a few moments as I watched, then they too became still and silent. I knew, in that moment, that a part of Henry was there watching us all and I knew he was smiling with his dancing blue eyes.

It was a perfect farewell party and everyone shared their thoughts and memories of Henry and told how good he had made them feel. How he had lit up their lives in some special way.

Before I left, Hugh Jenkins approached me and said, "Can I have a word with you before you go, Mr. Fanshaw? Mr. MacFarlane has left you his books. There aren't many—perhaps thirty or so—not of any great monetary value, you understand?" I was choked, but managed to say,

"He couldn't have left me anything better!" I meant every word of it!

The solicitor told me that they would be clearing the house over the next two days as Henry's son was flying back to Australia on Friday. I arranged to meet them at the house next day to collect my legacy.

Henry never ceased to amaze me!

Frances and I were making our way back to the car. As we walked under the oak tree I ran my fingers along the rough bark on the strong trunk. We were both lost in our own thoughts. Frances said in a dreamy sort of voice, "From a great oak…." And in a similar strange voice I heard myself say, "A little accountant grew…."

We turned towards each other in surprise and laughed. Frances said, "These were Henry's words, weren't they?"

We both knew that this was so!

EPILOGUE

The following eighteen months brought continued growth to James Fanshaw. Many changes occurred. He sold his flat and moved to a delightful little house near the canal. It had a beautiful garden which he enjoyed greatly and he was given much helpful advice from his old friend Harry Boswell. The garden reached right down to the edge of the canal, so he frequently had several ducks lazing on his lawn. He placed a wooden seat at this end of the garden and he liked to sit here and read or just think or meditate. Passing barges, especially in the summer months, were a source of interest and entertainment.

The house itself was so much more than just a place to live. It was a real home. It was light and bright and felt very peaceful. It was uncluttered and contained only things that James liked to have around.

He did not live alone any more. He shared his home with Anna, a sleek, smoky grey, greyhound.

Fiona from his office had asked if he would be interested in giving a home to this dog—a former racing greyhound, who was unwanted now that she could no longer win races or produce pups for her owner.

James agreed to meet the unwanted Annabelle and fell in love with her at once. It was a mutual affair and there was no discussion to be made. It was a union made in heaven! The day James took Anna back to their new home by the canal was one of the happiest in James Fanshaw's life so far.

One day, when out walking, James found himself in Oak Walk. He still came this way occasionally but seldom sat on the bench. There was a new bench here now—slightly higher than the rest—a better height for arthritic hips and knees. It faced away from the houses and was right underneath the great oak tree. This was the bench placed here in memory of Henry MacFarlane.

James sat down on Henry's bench, Anna sat by his side, her long, sleek velvety nose, resting on his knee. He closed his eyes and relaxed, breathing in the energy of the tree.

After a while, he became aware that someone had joined him on the bench. Anna had not moved, which seemed strange, as she usually reacted when anyone new came near.

James turned and looked at the young man seated beside him. He was very bronzed, with blonde hair, bleached by the sun. He was dressed like a back packer.

They greeted one another and as James looked at this man, he felt he recognised him. It was the eyes—these piercing blue eyes—Henry's eyes!

The young man said in a strong Australian accent, "This is my grandfather's bench—he used to live right over there."

James replied, " I knew your grandfather. We met under this tree a few years ago. He was a very special man. Someone I'll never forget."

The young Australian grinned widely, holding out a brown hand towards his neighbour, "I am James Henry MacFarlane—I'm delighted to meet you. Could you tell me about my grandfather?"

After about half an hour, the two men, a greyhound and a back pack headed off in the direction of the canal and a sudden breeze moved the leaves, high up in the oak tree....